ABOUT BLOODWATER

For readers who loved Attica Locke's Texas noir and Jesmyn Ward's Gulf Coast lyricism, Bloodwater delivers a white-knuckle story of a woman returning to Mississippi after her parents' death—only to find herself drawn into the orbit of a charismatic street preacher whose public salvation masks something far darker.

When Claudia Marston comes back to the Gulf Coast to settle her parents' estate, she expects grief, logistics, and closure. Instead, she finds a town quietly reordered—faith braided with charity, law enforcement, and local politics into a system that rewards obedience and punishes dissent.

As Claudia begins to see how moral authority is manufactured and protected, escape becomes less certain. Bloodwater moves between domestic thriller and civic indictment, tracing how corruption hides behind good works and how the Gulf Coast's history of storms, segregation, and extraction still determines who is protected—and who is expendable.

This is a novel about inheritance in all its forms—property, belief, violence, silence—and the cost of refusing the version of truth a town needs to survive.

Wholly Southern. Unsentimental. And unwilling to look away.

BLOODWATER

SCAN THE QR CODE BELOW TO JOIN THE
PREMIUM PULP FICTION SUBSTACK. YOU'LL GET
ACCESS TO EARLY CHAPTERS, PODCAST EPISODES,
NEW RELEASES, AND MEMBER PERKS.

YOU'LL ALSO GET EARLY ACCESS TO EVERY NEW
PREMIUM PULP FICTION TITLE.

NO SPAM. UNSUBSCRIBE ANYTIME.

IF THE CODE WON'T SCAN, PLEASE VISIT:
WWW.CITIZENONE.WORLD/PREMIUMPULP

BLOODWATER

BY
DOUGLAS STUART MCDANIEL

Premium Pulp Fiction Books
www.citizenone.world

SAVANNAH | OCEAN SPRINGS | BARCELONA

Copyright © 2026 Douglas Stuart McDaniel All rights reserved.

Thank you for purchasing an authorized edition of this book and for complying with copyright law. No part of this book may be reproduced, stored in a retrieval system, or transmitted by any means, electronic, mechanical, photocopying, recording, or otherwise, without written permission from the copyright holder.

This work is being published and distributed under the Premium Pulp Fiction imprint.

For ordering information or special discounts for bulk purchases, please contact Premium Pulp Fiction at: 1305 Barnard St #805 Savannah, GA 31401-6746.

Cover design and interior composition by Premium Pulp Fiction
with creative direction by the author.

Publisher's Cataloging-in-Publication data is available.

Print ISBN: 979-8-9935850-4-8

EBook ISBN: 979-8-9935850-5-5

Printed in the United States of America on acid-free paper

25 26 27 28 29 30 31 32   10 9 8 7 6 5 4 3 2 1

First Edition

DEDICATION

This book is for the people who carry others through broken seasons without calling it a virtue.

For those who understand that grief rarely arrives politely, that recovery is uneven, and that strength often looks like showing up with bad manners, great stories, and humor sharpened by experience. The kind of humor that doesn't minimize pain, but refuses to let it have the last word.

For the ones who know that places break people and people break places, and that loving either requires honesty rather than protection. Who accept that damage is not a failure of character, and that resilience is something practiced quietly, over time.

This book belongs to those who keep going after storms—personal and otherwise—not because they are heroic, but because stopping is not an option. To those who understand continuity, who rebuild without spectacle, who carry memory without smoothing it down.

It is offered in recognition of shared endurance, shared silence, and the strength that survives without explanation.

With affection,
Douglas Stuart McDaniel

Ocean Springs, Mississippi
March 2026

Although inspired by certain real places and fragments of regional and national public records spanning more than 50 years, this is a work of fiction. Characters, incidents, and dialogue are drawn from the author's imagination and are not intended to represent actual people or events. Any similarities are coincidental.

CONTENTS

DEDICATION VII
CONTENTS IX
PROLOGUE 1

ONE: BAYOU QUEENS AND BAD GIRLS 5
TWO: BAYOU HOUSE 13
THREE: 'GOULAS 25
FOUR: PASCAL'S WAGER 31
FIVE: MOONLIGHT 35
SIX: THUMPS AND SLAPS 41
SEVEN: GASLIGHT 45
EIGHT: SLIPPING AND FALLING 49
NINE: MAMA GHOST 53
TEN: SHAKEDOWN 57
ELEVEN: HARBOR OAKS 61
TWELVE: SAVED 65
THIRTEEN: POWERPOINT SAINTS 69
FOURTEEN: THE TOUSSAINTS 73
FIFTEEN: HERIFF BUCK 79
SIXTEEN: ECHOES 83
SEVENTEEN: BLOOD PRICE 91
EIGHTEEN: PRAY TO PLAY 97
NINETEEN: RITUAL OF SHADOWS 101
TWENTY: SIEGE 105
TWENTY-ONE: DOUBLING DOWN 113
TWENTY-TWO: THE JULEP ROOM 117
TWENTY-THREE: STING 127
TWENTY-FOUR: COPPER BOWLS 135
TWENTY-FIVE: JELLY JARS 145

AUTHOR'S NOTE 155
ABOUT THE AUTHOR 157

"Where you come from is gone, where you thought you were going to was never there, and where you are is no good unless you can get away from it."

— Flannery O'Connor, *Wise Blood*

PROLOGUE

This book began as a place. Not a plot, not a thesis—just a stretch of coast that refuses to behave the way brochures promise. Ocean Springs, Mississippi sits on the edge of the Gulf with its back half-turned toward America, the way some people sit in a room when they're listening but not agreeing. It is beautiful in the way working places often are: lived-in, compromised, weathered by money and storms and memory.

The bayou presses in close here. Water threads through everything—creeks, inlets, marsh grass, flood lines on old houses—quietly reminding you who's in charge. Beauty arrives unannounced: herons lifting from brackish water, live oaks leaning like they're tired of standing, light breaking open across the Sound at the wrong hour and still getting it right. None of it asks permission. None of it promises safety.

Poverty is present, but not performative. It doesn't announce itself. It settles. It shows up in patched roofs, in businesses that close without ceremony, in people who work two jobs and still speak carefully about money as if it might overhear them. The South knows this kind of arithmetic by heart. What it does not lack is pride—quiet, stubborn, and earned. People here know how to rebuild without calling it heroism. They know how to endure without pretending it makes them better than anyone else.

Hope survives differently in a place like this. It isn't loud. It isn't aspirational. It looks like staying. Like reopening. Like learning which storms to take seriously and which ones to ignore. It looks like neighbors who don't confuse help with charity, and who understand that resilience is not a slogan but a practiced skill.

Ocean Springs doesn't sell reinvention. It offers continuity. It keeps its losses close and its victories modest. It remembers everything the water carries in and takes back out again.

That refusal—to simplify, to clean itself up, to perform recovery—is what made this place demand a story.

And why this story could only begin here.

I didn't come here looking for a story. I came because places like this still tell the truth when you stay long enough.

Over the last decade, my life has been split across borders and time zones. I've lived and worked inside megaprojects, desert cities, speculative futures, and global institutions that speak fluently about progress while quietly erasing consequences. Somewhere along the way I became what I half-jokingly call a stateless nomad—American by birth, unmoored by profession, carrying home more as a habit than a fixed address.

Ocean Springs became one of those homes.

Barcelona became another.

That distance matters. Writing Bloodwater from a studio in Barcelona—an old city that has already survived empire, speculation, collapse, and reinvention—gave me the clarity I needed to look back at the American Gulf Coast without nostalgia or contempt. Distance sharpens memory. Heat does too. So does water that never forgets what's been poured into it.

This novel is not reportage, though it is informed by real economies, real power structures, and real patterns of violence and silence. It's not true crime, though the bones of it are there. It's Southern noir in the older sense: a story about money, proximity, complicity, and the quiet bargains people make to keep living where they live.

Bloodwater is one part of a larger body of work—what I've come to understand as a Southern noir trilogy.

PROLOGUE

The Dark Water Gospel documents Appalachia through an anthology of voices, crimes, folklore, and inherited memory—stories that never made it into official history because they were too inconvenient, too poor, or too local to matter to anyone in charge.

Defiance: A Reckoning with the Dream moves backward in time to Reconstruction-era Savannah, where the language of freedom collided with capital, race, and the machinery of American myth-making.

Bloodwater sits between them—geographically and morally—on the Gulf Coast, where tourism, extraction, old families, new money, and the residue of storms create a different kind of pressure.

These books are not sequels. They're adjacent rooms in the same house.

What binds them isn't plot, but gravity: how regions absorb violence, normalize it, and pass it down as culture. How respectability becomes a dialect of corruption. How water—rivers, coasts, floodplains—carries memory better than people do.

I didn't write Bloodwater to explain the South. I wrote it because I'm from it, even when I'm far away. Because leaving doesn't absolve you. Because some stories don't loosen their grip until you give them shape.

This is a novel about what stays submerged, and what eventually surfaces.

One
BAYOU QUEENS AND BAD GIRLS

Gulfport, Mississippi on a Saturday night, and the brewery smelled like hops, sweat, and the faint panic of people trying too hard to belong. The kind of place where craft beer was poured in pretentious flights, arranged like shot-glass jewels on lacquered boards, a world away from the longnecks and PBRs sweating on dive-bar pool tables just down Highway 49.

Out back, forklifts groaned as they loaded pallets of shrimp onto semi-trailers and rail cars under the halogen buzz of the port. Inside, refinery men and women in steel-toed boots cut stink-eyes at uppity grad students explaining "mouthfeel," everyone pretending they were part of the same conversation instead of two worlds colliding.

Claudia Marston watched them from a booth in the corner, wondering if she looked more like the grad students or the women in steel-toes. She wasn't sure which comparison made her feel lonelier.

The women carried the tang of crude and determination on their skin, hands marked with oil and wire, because at the Chevron Pascagoula Refinery or on the rigs farther out in the Gulf, women had been punching clocks and bending steel here for decades. Progress here looked like parity in the pits and the pipes—the same corroded halls, the same deadline contracts, the same heat clinging to the body.

They didn't need coffee stouts or peanut-butter ales to prove their worth; they carried refinery fire in their bones, a rhythm older and harder than the low thrum of the ragged cover band in the corner still clinging to Pearl Jam.

The crowd wanted to believe this was culture: citrus-forward IPAs with names stolen from dead pirates, sours that puckered harder than the first drag on a clove cigarette. It was the coastal South cosplaying as Brooklyn, poured into tulip glasses, swallowed under Edison bulbs and the hollow cheer of the bar.

The air itself still carried the scars of Hurricane Katrina—not just the salt rot in the walls, but the suspicion that lingered in every exchange, a civic PTSD in the twitch of people who had lost too much too fast and learned not to trust what came after.

Downtown brick façades bore faint waterlines like half-erased tattoos, reminders etched higher than any ladder could reach.

Behind the bar, a rusting FEMA trailer leaned like a relic, half-buried in sand and silt, its windows clouded, its story long abandoned but impossible to move. It stood as proof of what everyone already knew—that when the storm came, the institutions meant to protect them vanished, and the ones that showed up came late, took notes, and left with clipboards full of excuses. Around here, no one trusted the alphabet agencies anymore—FEMA, HUD, SBA—all acronyms that showed up late and left early. If the government came back, it would only be to tally losses, not to cover them. Claudia felt the distrust in her own skin, as if she'd inhaled it with the mildew—a wariness baked into every conversation, every sideways glance.

In the wreckage, a different kind of authority took root—men with voices louder than sirens, promising answers no agency could deliver. Their pulpits were parking lots and bridge overpasses, their scripture whatever kept the crowd listening. Claudia would soon learn to fear those voices most of all.

Outside, the town rattled with industrial chaos that never slept.

Shipyards coughed black smoke into the Gulf humidity, a constant bruise against the sky. The Seabee base spat out sailors every weekend—high-and-tight haircuts, hazard pay bulging their wallets, eyes hungry and restless. They came prowling through the bars like they were owed something, frustrated and half-feral, the kind of men who laughed too loud and stared too long. Some carried the brittle edge of entitlement, an undercurrent of grievance that bled into the way they talked about women—sex as conquest, intimacy as transaction. Online grievance had muscle here; it wore boots instead of avatars.

Freight trains screamed through downtown at ungodly hours, horns splitting the night, while convoys of eighteen-wheelers barreled down Highway 49 with cargo no one bothered to name, always bound for somewhere else, usually New Orleans. The government might have called it commerce, but here it looked more like extraction—goods leaving, nothing coming back but debt and new rules.

It all pressed in: the disaster's memory, the machinery, the endless churn of men and metal. Gulfport lived in that throb, somewhere between rebuilding and erasure, a town convinced that no institution was coming to save it, its pulse raw, suspicious, and dark as the tide.

The whole place had a rhythm: roughneck men drinking to forget the rigs, women on porches with cigarettes glowing like coronation candles, Bayou Queens in cutoffs and flip-flops who ruled their streets like thrones. They weren't waiting on anyone's permission—they ran tabs, ran rumors, ran whole families into or out of favor. Their dominion stretched from the bait shops to the beauty parlors, and every man in town knew it. Church steeples glowed just as bright as casino marquees, but it was the women who decided which prayers landed and which sins stuck.

The Gulf of Mexico was always there too—slick and silver by day, black and bottomless by night—swallowing men's secrets but never the women who carried them. Those stories clung like salt, passed down on porches and in kitchens, the real scripture of the coast. Queens, bad girls, saints, and hustlers—they kept the rhythm alive when the rigs and the preachers faltered, their laughter carrying farther than the hymns, sharper than the waves.

But there was always another preacher, waiting to turn that rhythm into new debts, into obedience. In towns like this, someone always rose from the swamp with a sermon and a ledger.

Claudia used to read those tides like scripture. Now she sat in this warehouse bar, realizing how far she'd drifted. In New York she'd lived twenty stories up, tracking volatility in foreign currencies, parsing charts and candlesticks the way some people read horoscopes. Here, volatility came in the form of black mold creeping up drywall and a storm season that never ended.

In 2020 alone, the Gulf Coast sat inside the cone of uncertainty ten different times, Ocean Springs sketched again and again into the hurricane cross-hairs before storms veered away. Three didn't: Cristobal, which made landfall in Louisiana that June but still drowned the coast in flooding rains; Delta, a Category 4 beast that tore into Louisiana in October and lashed Mississippi with surge and wind; and Zeta, which came screaming in late October with Category 3 winds, snapping power for days and chewing up piers, cars, and whole neighborhoods. The hurricane maps felt like prophecy charts, their narrowing lines as cryptic and fatalistic as any market signal, and Claudia found herself studying them with the same reverence she once gave to the rise and fall of markets. Here, the scripture wasn't about profit or loss—it was about whether her neighbors would have roofs come morning.

The brewery was an island in all that noise, a clean-swept warehouse trying too hard to look like Austin. Pendant lights glowed above long wooden tables, tealights trembling against laminated number cards, the whole place curated to feel intentional, safe, apart from the grit outside. By the time the band lurched into Jimmy Buffett, it wasn't just tragic anymore—it was sacrilege. Claudia felt bile rising. It wasn't just the music—it was the way the crowd whooped and sang along, voices cracking on Margaritaville as if the storm scars outside had never happened.

She pressed her palms flat against the table, the wood sticky from someone else's beer, and tried to remember why she'd come. In New York, irony was a currency—you could smirk at a kitsch lyric, sip your overpriced cocktail, and move on. Here, irony didn't play. Here, Buffett was gospel, a hymn to forgetting, to sandbars that never existed, to escape routes that always led back to the same broken piers.

Claudia's stomach turned because she knew the words too, every last one, and that was the part she couldn't forgive. She sat near the middle, stylish as hell and out of place, swirling a pale ale she didn't even like. Silk blouse, blood-red lipstick, sleeve tattoos hidden under the loose fabric. She was overdressed, overqualified, and over it—yet here she was, thirty-nine years old, back in Mississippi, trying to look interested in men who smelled faintly of diesel or desperation.

She told herself she came back only to sign probate papers and leave again. But even here, just a few miles from her old hometown of Ocean Springs, she could feel Bayou House clawing at her like an undertow.

Her armor was flawless: lipstick the shade of dried blood, heels that made her calves cut glass, and an expression that warned strangers she could dismantle them with a single glance. Beneath it all, though, was a brittleness. Something in her posture said: ask one wrong question and I might break.

The moderator—paunchy, overeager, the kind of man who mistook forced cheer for authority—clapped his hands for attention. "Alright, folks. Icebreaker. How did your last relationship end?"

Claudia thought: Jesus, could he sound more like a youth pastor running out of material?

Groans rolled through the room like waves in a storm. A man in a fishing shirt muttered, "Divorce court," drawing sympathetic laughter. A woman at the far end said, "He ghosted me after I redecorated his house," earning a chorus of oh-no-he-didn't gasps.

Then it was Claudia's turn.

She set down her glass, leaned in slightly, and spoke with the clarity of someone who knew exactly how absurd it would sound. "With guns, tear gas, a SWAT team, and a tank destroying my house."

For a moment, silence. Then nervous laughter rippled through the group—ha-ha, what a joker, what a quirky way to say bad breakup.

The silence felt familiar, like the breath before a sermon—that charged pause where someone dangerous was about to tell you who you were and what it would cost to change. But Claudia didn't smile. She just held their eyes, one by one, until the laughter thinned into uncertainty.

She'd seen the same look in Manhattan boardrooms when a deal went bad—laughter first, then the silence when everyone realized the numbers weren't coming back.

Fear lived in that pause.

From across the table, a woman in jeans and a fitted T-shirt leaned back, smirking. Badge clipped to her belt, the unmistakable air of law enforcement. She raised her beer and said: "She ain't lying. I was there."

Tables went dead quiet. Forks froze mid-air. Someone at the end of the table crossed themselves. Someone else checked the exit. A glass clinked too hard against the wood.

Claudia let the silence breathe. Then she tilted her head, smirk curling at the edge of her lips. "Let me back up..."

The room was still locked—beers half-raised, mouths hanging open, everyone wondering if she was crazy, cursed, or the most interesting woman they'd ever sat across from.

Claudia Marston knew she could be all three.

Stylish, brittle, carrying too much history for her frame. The kind of woman who ran from Ocean Springs a decade ago, thinking New York boardrooms and buttoned-up men could smother her appetite for chaos. But ghosts don't stay buried, and neither do bad habits.

Under the silk blouse and corporate armor, Claudia was a bad girl tattooed with the story of her life. Her left arm was a full sleeve, a tide pool of memories inked into skin: blue crabs and skeleton keys twined together, a nod to her father's old bus driver keys, heavy on a brass ring. One summer, her mother hurled them into the bayou during a fight, where they sank into the fish-guts muck. She had to dive for them, emerging covered in slime, cursing the whole family. That argument detonated an entire weekend trip. Claudia had it inked so she'd never forget what chaos looked like in miniature.

A tattoo of a skeletal flamingo perched near her elbow, a Halloween memory in neon pink and bone white. Her mother had a soft spot for tacky flamingos, even sticking one in the yard every October, dressed up like death in a feathered shroud. Claudia wore it like a badge: absurdity and grief in one bird.

Near her forearm, an inked armadillo—a private joke about her mother's love for grotesque mascots. Once, she'd plopped the real thing—a taxidermy "possum on the half shell"—onto the kitchen counter just to horrify guests. It stayed there for years, a family mascot of dysfunction.

Behind all of it, a line of box turtles, etched in muted greens, crawling up toward her shoulder. Not sea turtles, not anything exotic—just the humble box turtles that wandered up from the woods every summer, looking for scraps. She had fed them all her life. She wore them now as quiet witnesses, the ones who always came back, even when she didn't.

The sleeve wasn't fashion. It was inheritance, rebellion, confession. A portable armory of ghosts.

In Manhattan, she'd tracked currencies tick by tick. Here, it was the tattoos that flickered: crabs clawing, flamingos smirking, turtles plodding.

And under it all she could still smell the marsh, the one she swam in every summer, the one her father used as his backdrop for Scotch and cigars. The tattoos weren't art so much as memory pinned to flesh.

That's what the men across the brewery tables couldn't see when she dropped her line about tanks and tear gas. They saw silk and lipstick. They didn't see the muck of the bayou, the skeletal flamingo, or the turtles she fed and then abandoned. They didn't see Ocean Springs written all over her skin.

So she came back—to the haunted house her parents left her, to the bayou that watched everything, to a town that had a long memory and a short fuse. She came back to ghosts carved into woodwork, to turtles waiting at the marsh's edge, to memories as heavy as the humidity. She came back with her guard down, telling herself she was only here to sign papers, pack boxes, and leave again.

But the bayou didn't care about paperwork. It pulled at her like a current, dragging her back to faces she thought she'd outrun. One of them was waiting, sharpening his sermons, hungry for her story. She didn't know his name yet. Soon she would.

Two
BAYOU HOUSE

Claudia had become intimately familiar with Delta's seat maps and the stale smell of airports. She had endured months of back-and-forth, bleeding money on last-minute tickets and attorney fees, circling probate like a vulture. Her parents died three months apart—cancer for her father, and something her mother called "little bastard syndrome," despite knowing its clinical name for a short while—Lewy Body Syndrome. The same disease that had stolen Robin Williams and countless other bright minds. Claudia thought her mother's name for it was just as fitting: a bastard illness that unravels the person you love into fragments until you're left talking to a ghost in real time.

She'd learned the cadence of death paperwork: certified mail, signatures in blue ink, a courthouse clerk who stapled like she meant it. Probate had a smell, too—toner and old carpet—nothing like the marsh, but just as relentless in the way it clung.

Now she was back again, driving a rental car over the bridge into Ocean Springs, and the town rose out of the marsh the same as always: stubborn, humid, unrepentant. Moss-draped live oaks hunched over cracked streets. Over at Ocean Springs Harbor, half-sunk shrimp boats leaned against rotten docks, their hulls tattooed with salt and neglect.

Tiny compared to Biloxi's massive Back Bay fleet, trawlers still tied up here, especially during shrimping season. Neon beer signs flickered outside sagging bars where roughnecks drank away shipyard wages. The old downtown carried a whiff of paint and polish for tourists, but the rust and rot were never more than an arm's length away.

More Katrina-era FEMA trailers lay along rural highways, canted at odd angles like molars about to pop.

To the west, Gulfport's cranes still clawed at the sky, containers stacked like children's blocks, belching diesel into the sticky air.

Claudia rolled down the window and drank it all in—the industrial mayhem, the fish rot, the gasoline—and it settled in her chest like an old wound reopening.

Lower Manhattan was far removed from all of this: her home was Hudson Yards now, her office just steps away—once a shipyard, now gentrified glass and steel stacked against the river. Down here was another world entirely. In New York, crises were decimal points and deadlines; here, crisis had texture: rust, tide, heat.

Bayou House, the family home for generations, waited at the end of a shaded road, crouched behind a curtain of trees that felt more like a warning than a welcome. Her inheritance—and her sister's. Burdensome now. Creaking and swollen with humidity, perched near the forgotten ruins of Fort Maurepas like a sentry no one remembered. This was the place where the French planted their first flag in Mississippi in 1699, a wooden fort hacked out of the swamp to keep watch over the Gulf. Long gone—just a plaque and a scar in the earth—but at night the bluff still sounded like wood on water and boots in mud. Bayou House had been built a century later on the bluff above, and Claudia always thought the boards creaked like they remembered too.

The porch boards answered her steps with a damp complaint. The front door stuck at the latch—swollen, stubborn—and when it finally gave, a breath of cool rot unrolled from the dark like something exhaled.

She studied the house the way she used to study quarterly reports—looking for what was missing, not what was there. Every board had a number attached in her head, every repair a calculation she didn't want to make. Bayou House wasn't inheritance. It was liability dressed as nostalgia.

Bullet divots scalloped the siding by the kitchen window—old family jokes said "hunting possum," but she knew better. The house wore its history like acne scars.

Shutters dangled loose, porch boards warped, paint blistered into scales. The place seemed to breathe with its own pulse, to watch her more than she watched it. Every trip back had been a negotiation—her parents' ghosts pressing against the walls, asking what the hell took her so long. Dad with his Scotch and cigars, his legs dangling off the end of the pier, surrounded by the marsh. Mom hosting a fish fry for the neighbors. Neither of them here anymore, and yet both of them everywhere she looked.

Mildew filmed the hall mirror. The HVAC wheezed a tired, humid warning of imminent collapse. From somewhere inside, a slow drip kept time—a metronome for the kind of decisions you can't walk away from.

She set a palm to the jamb. The wood was soft. The house felt alive in the wrong way.

She wasn't ready to go inside yet. Not tonight. Bayou House crouched behind its curtain of trees, and Claudia knew she wasn't alone in its shadow. A glow pressed through the warped blinds upstairs. She knew her sister Caroline was home tonight.

Of course she was. Caroline had become part of the house the way vines claimed the porch rails—impossible to separate without tearing something down. Caroline, once the wild twin, the barefoot one who used to vanish for days with boys and guitars, had turned into the dutiful daughter when it counted, spoon-feeding Mom through her fog and hauling Dad to chemo when no one else would. Divorced now, no kids, just canvases stacked against the walls and jars of gummies in the kitchen. She still smoked too much weed, painted until dawn, and talked big about turning Bayou House into an artist colony—as if she could scrub grief out with turpentine and murals.

Claudia could already hear the judgment in the clink of Caroline's brush jars: not bitter, exactly—more like a ledger kept in pencil.

Claudia could picture her in there now, barefoot in one of Dad's old flannels, hair twisted into a bandanna, porch door propped open to let the smoke drift into the trees. Caroline always carried herself like she belonged here, like she had roots where Claudia had only scars.

Roots versus scars—that was the axis they spun on.

The sight of those lights made Claudia's chest ache with equal parts guilt and resentment. She wasn't ready for Caroline's easy claim to the place, or for the look she knew was waiting—half reproach, half welcome, all certainty. Not tonight.

She let the door ease shut before the hinges could complain, the house settling behind her like a creature deciding not to bite—yet.

So she drove past the house, deeper into the old part of town, where the asphalt broke into gravel and the air thickened with the smell of pine.

• • •

Claudia loved Bellande Cemetery—believed to be the oldest in Ocean Springs. She parked on the grass edge of Dewey Avenue near the bay in eastern Old Ocean Springs. The place dated back to the LaFontaine family plot on Joseph Bellande's nineteenth-century farm. Much later it became a neighborhood burying ground.

A tangle of wrought-iron gates and toppled stones marked the place, some so old the names had washed away. Live oaks spread their branches like cathedral vaults, roots cracking marble slabs. Angels leaned at odd angles, their faces veiled in moss. A Confederate obelisk rose near the center, ringed by crumbling family plots, while closer to the bayou the poorer graves lay under simple wooden crosses that had long since lost their paint.

The dead generally stayed put, even through Hurricane Katrina. That was their kindness. Claudia wandered past them all, her heels sinking into the damp ground, until she found the new stones that stopped her in her tracks. Her parents lay side by side now, the grass still raw and torn from the burial. The markers were clean, the granite unweathered, too new to belong in a place like this.

New granite against old ground—another entry in her liminal ledger. She stood there a long time, hands clasped in front of her like a child in church, though none of them had ever believed much in prayer. Her father had been a lapsed Catholic, the kind who kept a rosary tucked in a drawer but never darkened the door of a parish after his own father's funeral. Her mother had been harder, sharper—a nonbeliever forged by years of alcoholic abuse at the hands of Claudia's grandfather. For her, church was another place where men in collars pretended to be holy while covering for the unholy.

And Claudia herself—she was an atheist in full, not out of rebellion but out of conviction. If God was real, she thought, then he was cruel, or indifferent, or both. Cancer chewing through her father, Lewy Body Syndrome stealing her mother piece by piece until her laughter flickered in and out like bad reception—that was all the evidence she needed. A merciful God would never script that kind of ending.

Even so, the oaks made their own cathedral, and she stood quiet inside it.

The arguments, the slammed doors, the family drama that had defined so much of her leaving—all of it dissolved in the hush of this spot. She wanted grace, she wanted peace, and for once she didn't need the details of how it all went down. Cancer and Lewy body dementia had been merciless enough. The fights didn't matter anymore.

She rubbed the Icelandic tattoo on her left forearm, the one she'd gotten in Reykjavik years ago after drinking too much Brennivín and promising herself she would always honor her mother's wish. A Viking knotwork circle, inked in black and blue, a reminder of fire on water. The burning boat she had promised to set afloat in the bayou, her mother's wild wish for a pagan funeral.

"I'll do it," she said to the stones, and to the house by extension. "I'll set the fire."

"I'm sorry," she continued, though she wasn't sure to which of them, or for what. Her father, for not being there at the end. Her mother, for the funeral she hadn't yet given her. Or herself, for still standing here trying to believe in something, anything, even as she knew there was nothing waiting in the dark but memory. The promise of that Viking funeral still burned bright, vivid as the smell of salt marsh in summer. But tonight, all she could do was stand in the silence, let her fingers press into the carved granite, and hope they understood.

She let her fingers drift across the names, traced the grooves as if touch alone could bring back voices, laughter, the smell of her father's cigars and her mother's casseroles cooling on the counter.

The granite was still sun-warm. Her fingers came away with a green dust of lichen. For the first time since stepping off the plane, her breath slowed.

The dead had a way of grounding you in this town.

The living were the problem—especially the ones with keys.

Among the living, Ocean Springs had a short memory and a quick temper. But the cemetery reminded her of another truth: the land itself never forgot. What Claudia needed now was a drink—and the kind of sisterhood that came poured over ice and wrapped in smoke.

• • •

Claudia left the dead to their unsettling silence and drove back toward downtown, following the curve of Porter Avenue where the neon signs flared like beacons. Frankie's bar glowed at the corner, a low-slung building with chipped paint, the kind of place that never needed to advertise because everyone already knew where to go when they wanted to drink too much and say too much. A battered jukebox thumped out Pink Floyd's "Hey You," leaking the lyrics into the street through warped wooden walls, and cigarette smoke hung above the doorway like a permanent fog.

She pushed inside and was hit with the familiar mix: old beer soaked into wood, fryer grease that had never quite left, and the clean sharpness of lemon rinds dropped into whiskey glasses. The place was dim but alive, voices overlapping, pool balls cracking, laughter with a mean edge. This was Frankie's kingdom, and every barstool, every warped floorboard bent to her rule.

Frankie stood behind the counter, tall and wiry, with the kind of posture that dared you to underestimate her. Black hair streaked with silver pulled into a knot, her forearms corded with muscle as she wiped down a pint glass. A cigarette dangled from the side of her mouth, and when she spoke it was in a voice so low and deliberate that you leaned in without meaning to.

Once upon a time she hadn't just run a bar—she'd run Biloxi. Back before Katrina, when casinos still floated on barges tethered to piers, Frankie had been the one to light them up. Sequins on her shoulders, chip trays balanced against her hip, she'd worked the floor until sunrise, the queen of smoke and neon. The underworld pulsed around her: high-rollers from New Orleans, hustlers with mob ties, shrimp boat captains trying to wash cash through slot machines. She knew every pit boss, every dealer, every trick the house pulled to keep the suckers playing.

That was before the mainland hotels rose up like fortresses, before the corporations took over and bleached the grit out of the business. Frankie walked away, cashed in her chips, and opened this bar instead. Smaller, dirtier, but hers.

Now she reigned over it with the same no-nonsense intensity, trading roulette wheels for whiskey bottles. And when Claudia stepped through the door, Frankie's eyes landed on her like the ball finding its slot on the wheel—no surprise, no hesitation, just inevitability.

Frankie clocked the marsh salt still clinging to Claudia's hair and the courthouse stress on her shoulders.

"Well, well. Manhattan comes crawling back." Frankie smirked, sliding a glass of bourbon across the bar before Claudia could ask. "You still know how to drink, or did they beat that out of you up north?"

At the far end of the bar, hunched over a beer and a shot, was Dottie. If Frankie was a queen, Dottie was a warlord. Sixty going on indestructible, her gray hair chopped short and wild, her biker vest stitched with patches from rallies all over the South. A pair of aviator sunglasses sat on the counter next to her ashtray, even though the sun had been down for hours. Her hands were thick, scarred from fights and bail skips she'd dragged in herself, and she smoked like every drag was both punctuation and threat.

When she saw Claudia, she barked a laugh, smoke curling from her lips. "Well, shit. Look at you. All fancy in silk and heels, like you forgot this town's built on swamp mud and bad decisions."

Claudia smiled despite herself. "Still running bonds, Dottie?"

"Still saving assholes from themselves, one at a time." Dottie raised her glass in a mock toast. "And charging 'em interest, of course."

Frankie leaned on the bar, her eyes narrowing with that half-amused, half-suspicious look she wore like eyeliner. "So. What brings you back? More lawyers?"

Claudia smirked but didn't bite right away. She let the bourbon burn its way down first.

"Claudia's still chasing ghosts, I bet," Dottie said, amused. "Or one of her bad boys."

"No bad boys yet," Claudia quipped.

"Yet," Frankie said, arching an eyebrow. "That word always gets you in trouble."

Claudia toyed with the glass, tracing the rim with one finger. "I came back to settle the estate. Sign papers, pay off debts, maybe sell the place if I can get anyone to take it. Bayou House isn't exactly prime real estate these days. Probate's a mess. Windstorm claim denied, taxes overdue, and some LLC keeps sliding cash offers under the door like I'm desperate."

Frankie's mouth twitched. "Cash makes a lot of folks sentimental."

"About other people's houses," Claudia said.

Frankie gave a low laugh. "You'd sell your momma and daddy's place just like that? Walk away like none of it mattered?"

Not an accusation—more a temperature check.

Claudia bristled. "It's not home anymore. It's rot and mold and memories I didn't ask to inherit. I don't need a haunted house to remind me of what I lost."

She didn't say: the house is watching, and I don't like what it sees.

She heard it herself as the words left her mouth—how the clipped Manhattan cadence she'd spent a decade perfecting was softening, syllables dragging into the low-country drawl of her childhood. Each sentence pulled her further from New York's boardrooms and closer to the humid front porches she thought she'd outrun. By the end, she didn't sound like a woman defending her career-polished veneer. She sounded like a daughter arguing on a bayou dock, like she'd never left at all.

"There she is," Frankie said softly, admiring her old friend. "Girl I remember. Not the one in the suit."

For a moment, Frankie didn't speak. She studied Claudia the way she used to study a roulette wheel, waiting for the ball to land.

"Selling's clean," she said at last. "Keeping's work."

"Keeping is drowning," Claudia answered. "Selling is oxygen."

"So which is it gonna be?" She asked finally. "Cash out, wipe your hands of Ocean Springs for good? Or you here to exorcise the demons that keep dragging you back?"

Claudia met her eyes. There was no smirk this time, just the weight of exhaustion.

"I don't know," she said. "Maybe both. Maybe neither. Maybe I just need one more goddamn drink before I figure it out."

She didn't add: Caroline will have an opinion.

Frankie poured it without another word.

The jukebox flipped to another track, the room buzzing with laughter and clinking bottles, but the question hung in the air like static. Claudia didn't answer right away. She just sipped the bourbon Frankie had placed in front of her and let the fire burn down her throat, tasting the past in every drop.

Somewhere behind her sternum, the house shifted—imagined or not—and she felt it like weather.

These two women—Frankie with her sharp edges, Dottie with her storm-front energy—were the first anchors she had in a town that still felt like it might swallow her whole. Two hurricanes, different names, same season: the kind of women that blew roofs off houses but also cleared the air. She could already feel the barometric drop.

And then the door opened, letting in a wash of warm night air laced with magnolia and cigarette smoke. Lila swept in like she belonged to another world entirely. Barefoot in loose linen pants, hair twisted into a careless knot, a yoga mat slung over her shoulder as if she'd wandered straight from a sunrise class into this dive bar. She carried incense on her skin, that sweet resinous smell, like she'd dragged half a temple with her.

"Speak of the goddess," Frankie muttered, smirking as she poured a tonic into a highball.

Dottie grunted. "Here comes the incense brigade."

But Lila just smiled, unbothered, like she always did. She glided to the bar, set her mat against the stool, and kissed Claudia on both cheeks. "I felt the shift in the air," she said, eyes bright. "I knew you were back."

Claudia let out a breath she hadn't realized she was holding. "How? You got some clairvoyant hot line I don't know about?"

Lila tapped her heart with two fingers. "Doesn't take a Ouija board. Some of us pay attention."

Dottie snorted, dragging from her cigarette. "What she means is the town's been buzzing ever since you set foot on the bridge. Ocean Springs don't keep secrets long."

Before Claudia could answer, another figure pushed through the doorway behind Lila. The room shifted—conversations dipped, a few heads turned. Caroline stepped into the bar like she owned the floorboards, smoke trailing from the joint pinched between her fingers. She wore cutoffs and one of their father's old flannel shirts, sleeves rolled to the elbow, bare feet in scuffed leather sandals. A canvas tote slung over her shoulder spilled brushes and paint rags.

Her eyes found Claudia's instantly, sharp and unsparing, twin mirrors that had seen too much. Caroline exhaled a long stream of weed smoke, let it curl above the jukebox where Pink Floyd warbled out its ache.

"Well, look who the Gulf dragged back," she said, voice raspy but steady. "Figured I'd find you here before I found you at the house."

Claudia's throat tightened. She'd prepared herself for ghosts tonight, not for Caroline in the flesh.

Frankie arched an eyebrow, sliding Caroline a beer without asking. "Twins in the same room again. Must be the apocalypse."

Dottie barked a laugh. "Or the second coming. Depending on which one's holier."

Caroline ignored them, eyes still locked on Claudia. She took another drag, stubbed the joint out in Dottie's ashtray, and leaned across the bar. "You gonna say hello, sis? Or you just came back to haunt me like the rest of 'em?"

Not a bite to draw blood—just a nip to see if Claudia still flinched.

The silence stretched, thick with smoke and memory. Claudia finally picked up her glass, raised it in a half-toast, and said, "Hello, Caroline."

"Hello," Caroline answered, softening a notch. Then, business: "Lawyer called me today. Tax bill's uglier than last month."

"I know," Claudia said. "I'll cover it."

Caroline's smile was quick and crooked. "Or you could sell and make it someone else's problem."

There it was—the lever.

"I'm considering it," Claudia said.

"Consider faster," Caroline replied, not unkind. "The house eats slow, but it eats."

The room seemed to lean closer, waiting for trouble. Caroline gave a crooked grin, stepped forward, and pulled her sister into a hug that smelled of turpentine, weed, and marsh air.

"Took you long enough," she murmured, squeezing tight before letting go. Then, just as quick, she dug into her tote and pulled out a crumpled Ziploc, holding up a red gummy between two fingers like a peace offering. "Want one? Cherry. Makes probate court almost tolerable."

Claudia laughed, the sound jagged but real. "I'll stick with bourbon. At least that poison's predictable."

"Suit yourself," Caroline said, popping it into her mouth and chewing slow, eyes never leaving her twin.

Judgment tucked itself back into her pocket, like a pocketknife—useful, not personal.

The tension eased. Frankie snorted. "Jesus, the Marston girls in one room again. Somebody better bolt the doors."

Dottie raised her glass. "And hide the menfolk."

Lila smiled, watching the exchange with that unshakable calm she carried everywhere. She set her tonic down, bracelets clinking soft as wind chimes, and laid a hand on Claudia's shoulder. "See? The world didn't end, baby. You're among sisters now."

Her voice carried the kind of peace you only earn after surviving fire. Everybody in town remembered Lila's first husband—the mean drunk who used to bark her name loud enough for the neighbors to hear. Then one day he was gone. Packed up, moved on, folks said.

But Ocean Springs had its own math. Men like him didn't just "move on." They ended up in the marsh, or fed to the gators, or swallowed whole by the Gulf. No body ever turned up. No one filed a missing persons. The law didn't ask.

Dottie never talked about it, but there'd been a night years back when she showed up at Frankie's with blood on her boots and a look that dared anyone to pry. Lila never said a word, just kept on teaching yoga, welding bracelets, breathing smoke and incense into every space she entered.

She wasn't a victim. She was proof. In Ocean Springs, the women looked out for each other, and some men just… disappeared.

Out beyond the neon, the house waited—patient, hungry, and listening.

Three
'GOULAS

Caroline had insisted on brunch, dragging Claudia into the bright crush of downtown Ocean Springs on a Saturday that smelled of chicory coffee and fried oysters. As they sipped bloody marys, they watched as 'goula matriarchs, born and raised in nearby Pascagoula, spun their Mercedes into narrow parking spaces. These women ruled the town, carrying themselves like gulf-side royalty, hair lacquered against the Gulf humidity. They wore pearls by day, diamonds by night. Claudia had almost forgotten the choreography: the linen, the pearls, the lineage rehearsed like scripture.

Squinting, Claudia recognized Mavis Ann Dupré. "I thought ol' Mavis was dead, Caroline."

Her sister didn't even look up. "Dead? Please. She's like a cockroach in Chanel. Somebody swore she drowned in her own pool back in '09, but you know Mavis—she just quit paying the pool boy."

Claudia watched the woman glide past in white linen. Aristocracy carved out of bayou mud, pretending their china cabinets could hold back the mildew—and the palmetto bugs that scurried across silver platters and soup tureens when the lights went out. She remembered enough from childhood to never say "cockroach" in good company.

You softened it with "palmetto," the way you renamed sin as mischief.

Their menfolk were cut from ship steel and sweat. Some barked orders on tugboats, others strutted in seersucker, all convinced the tides answered to them. The covenant was clear: gossip for the women, silence for the men.

That was how Ocean Springs stayed stitched. Tourists clogged the rest: sunburned, drunk before noon, blasting Kenny Chesney and Lee Greenwood from Bluetooth speakers on their golf carts. Ghosts floated too—homeless men in overcoats despite the ninety-degree heat, women with dolls swinging on strings. They were tolerated like mildew in sheet rock: everyone saw it, no one admitted it. A gospel duo on Government Street spilled half-tuned harmony into the air.

The town hummed—half genteel, half lawless. You could see it in the pastel facades downtown, freshly painted over crumbling plaster, and in the rainbow-colored umbrellas strung high above the pedestrian cross streets, a canopy meant for postcards and Instagram selfies.

Boutiques and wine bars had crept into spaces once filled with hardware stores and secondhand shops, a cosmetic face lift sold as progress. But just beyond the fairy lights and planter boxes, tents and shopping carts pressed into the alleys, the unhoused edged further out each season by codes enforcement and climbing rents. Across the South, the same contradiction repeated itself: revitalization pitched as rebirth, nostalgia packaged for visitors, while working-class families slipped beneath the waterline. The surface gleamed, but the undertow still dragged.

Caroline did most of the talking, her voice spilling over mimosas about insurance claims and LSU football games. Claudia let her, answering in half-smiles, her eyes tugged toward the edges: the peeling paint on awnings, the flicker of the church sign across the street, the ragged cluster outside the old Rexall pharmacy.

Pushing her glass aside, Caroline let the lime wedge sink into murky red. She wasn't looking at Claudia, just out the window where the humidity glazed the street.

"You know what it was?" She said, her tone flat. "It was so damn funny the way Daddy would try to light his cigar after chemo. His hands shook so bad he couldn't keep the match steady. I'd have to cup my palms around it, like I was shielding a holy flame. And she—" Caroline's mouth twitched, almost a smile, but not quite. "She would be halfway gone by then, talking to shadows like they were old neighbors. Calling me by her sister's name. Half the time she thought I was someone else. So, I'd have to be two people at once. Daughter and stranger."

She shrugged, as if filing it away in some mental cabinet. "That's what the last couple of years was. Holding the match. Answering to names that weren't mine. Watching both of them leave us in pieces."

The words weren't bitter, not even resentful—just factual, like receipts spread on the table. Yet Claudia felt the sting anyway.

"So, I tried to keep the bills straight," Caroline added, shifting in her chair. "Kept the house from falling in, because somebody had to."

Claudia realized she had nothing to offer back, no memory to place beside Caroline's. She'd been on planes, in offices, wrapped up in men her parents distrusted. The bad choices they'd shaken their heads over had followed her like a reputation, until "Claudia" became shorthand for the one who couldn't be counted on.

They'd never forgiven her taste in men—the addicts, the bikers, the drifters and charmers who could turn every Sunday dinner into a battlefield. Caroline had filed those names away like debts, and their parents had agreed. Branded the black sheep long before she'd even left town. And still, part of her wanted to argue—to say she'd had her reasons, that New York had been its own kind of survival.

But Caroline had carried the burden of family, and everyone knew it. She finally looked at her sister, eyes clear but rimmed with years of sleepless nights.

"So don't come at me like you know what those months were. You weren't here."

She said it without malice. Just the plain truth, and Claudia had to sit with it.

That's when the commotion started. A sunburned man shouting at two locals—men too old to be called boys, but still cruel for sport.

Caroline tensed beside her, the way she always did when strangers raised their voices in public—disorder felt contagious. They jeered, and when his fist twitched, someone's iced coffee burst on the sidewalk.

Phones came up.

Caroline muttered, "Lord, not again." And from the corner, the silence bent. Brother Ray. He wasn't tall—five foot nothing—but he moved with a strange authority, part preacher, part hustler, part carnival act that refused to close. Bald head gleaming, snake tattoo curling up one arm, the straps of a floral sarong knotted with fishing line.

He cut straight into the quarrel, voice booming: "Peace, children! You don't fight where the Lord laid oysters and shrimp. Not here on God's glittering bayou!"

And damned if the fight didn't pause. The locals muttered and drifted off. The ragged man followed Ray like a disciple. Others clustered too, thrift-store rags brushing against him as though he carried a flame.

People on the sidewalk glanced, then looked away. Same reflex as an HOA board—see the mess, say nothing, pray it doesn't park on your street.

That afternoon, Claudia saw him again at the gas station. The kind with cracked pumps, a flickering sign that read JESUS SAVES, and a counter wiped too clean, as if trying to erase what passed across it. It reminded Claudia of the way neighbors used to bite their tongues on the porch when her parents fought—the practiced silence of a town that always looked away.

Ray Broussard perched on a milk crate, his sarong riding high, laughing like a trickster god with a cigarette burned to the filter. He was built narrow through the hips, sinewy as river cane, a prison-pale body inked in jailhouse blues and half-healed scripture. His scalp was shaved to stubble, scalp scars catching the fluorescent light like thin silver fish. Sun had leathered his neck and shoulders to the color of boiled crawfish shells. A rope of cheap wooden beads hung where a clerical collar might have been, and his feet were bare, soles black with asphalt dust.

His flock orbited, waiting for his patter. When he spotted Claudia, he lit up.

"Well, look at this here queen," he crowed, loud enough for everyone. "Fresh from far lands. You shine like you've been kissed by death and deliverance. Come sit here with your new family."

His stories poured out like cheap whiskey—how he'd drowned twice and come back, how Jesus rode shotgun with him through Biloxi, how he once turned whiskey into gasoline just to keep a church bus running. Locals called him Brother Ray.

Nonsense, all of it, but Claudia found herself laughing for the first time in months, and leaned closer. The raw magnetism was undeniable. At the register, a clerk wiped the counter in small, nervous circles. A nurse in scrubs counted out two dollars for gas, eyes cast downward.

Claudia caught the look, the silence thick as humidity. Nobody said what they were thinking: what the hell is wrong with you, letting this man hold court here? She didn't notice Dottie until the voice came low at her shoulder.

"Don't," Dottie said. "He's poison. He'll drink you dry and leave you with nothing but ash."

Claudia wanted to laugh it off, to say she'd seen worse. But some part of her—the part still aching from Caroline's accounting—leaned toward the circle anyway, as if Ray's chaos might take her in where family never had. Ray grinned like he'd heard every word. He raised his arms, sarong straps fluttering.

"Even poison can be medicine, if you know how to take it!"

Her laugh rose, too bright, too brittle, until it tangled with the flock's howl and became indistinguishable from the rest.

Four
PASCAL'S WAGER

The house had been closed up too long, and it smelled like sweet rot—an old perfume of wallpaper glue, lacquered wood, and humidity that refused to die. Claudia opened every window she could wrestle free, fighting swollen frames that stuck as if they resented her touch. She built crooked towers of boxes: medical bills, court papers, yellowed insurance policies, and church bulletins brittle enough to crumble in her hands. Their parents had saved everything and nothing—years of clutter without a single note that explained what to do now.

Caroline padded in barefoot, iced tea sweating in her hand. She looked around the dining room stacked high with boxes. "This feels like purgatory," she said.

"Appropriate," Claudia answered, dragging another carton into place. "Daddy probably thinks he's in purgatory right now, waiting on God's tap on the shoulder."

It was the story he loved telling when they were kids—that back in upstate Mississippi, he believed God would one day single him out and demand he become a priest. He'd laugh about how he'd dodged it, how he'd outrun the shoulder tap with a wife, two babies, and a job at the yard. But toward the end, their father began hedging his bets. The French had a name for it—Pascal's Wager. Live as if God exists, just in case He does. He sat straighter in the pew at St. Alphonsus, mouthing prayers half-remembered from boyhood, glancing at the crucifix like a man squinting at an old contract. He didn't believe so much as insure himself, slipping faith into his pocket like a lottery ticket, hoping it might pay out when the time came.

The old local Catholics called it a believer's bargain, but around towns like Ocean Springs, everyone knew the open secret: priests with their own sins, families whispering about pedophiles in the rectory, and forgiveness for sale if you just kept showing up in the pews.

Their mother never forgave herself for converting. Raised hard Baptist in Lower Alabama—L.A., as she referred to it, one blinking red light in the town and nothing but pine thickets around it—she'd run from her father's belt and bottle straight into a marriage. Pregnant and desperate, she'd knelt at an altar up in Canton and muttered her way through the Catholic vows. She despised the whole show, despised the irony of men preaching holiness with whiskey breath and fists bruised from Saturday night. Her father had tormented her twins whenever they visited, made their skin crawl with his vulgar jokes and wandering hands. The sisters learned early that religion, like family, could be a trap disguised as salvation.

The twins carried that history like a double helix. Claudia born at 11:58 p.m., Caroline at 12:01—three minutes older, one day apart. Parity was the rule: one won spelling bees, the other homecoming crowns. One escaped town, the other stayed and claimed ground. Even now, going through their parents' relics, each move felt measured against the other.

Faith, she decided, was just another investment portfolio—high risk, low liquidity, returns impossible to chart. Maybe Pascal had it half-right: you hedge your bets, not your heart. And maybe the sin wasn't disbelief at all. Maybe it was bad math.

Caroline shook her head, holding up a faded church bulletin. "Mama kept these? Why? She hated every minute she spent in that pew."

"Because she hated throwing anything away," Claudia said. "And because spite is its own scrapbook."

She was knee-deep in it when the whistle came from outside. Not a tune so much as a noise meant to announce presence. Both sisters turned at once.

Brother Ray leaned against the porch rail, toolbox in one hand, grocery sack in the other. His sarong had faded to the soft peach of a motel towel; sweat darkened the waistline. Tattoos—skulls, crosses, a weeping eye—crawled up his wiry arms. Up close his teeth showed the ruin of years: nicotine, neglect, and some hard-won charm that made the damage look deliberate. The smell of motor oil and bay water clung to him, as if he'd been baptized in both.

He grinned like the whole mess had been staged for his entrance. "Afternoon, queens," he said, bowing like an actor at curtain call. "Heard y'all settlin' up in here. Figured the Lord might want me to lend a hand. Thought you might need a strong back and a little divine intervention."

Caroline didn't even smile. She set her glass down with a sharp clink and said, "We don't need theatrics. We need deeds and account numbers." Her tone made it clear she considered him one more mess to sort, not a savior.

Before Claudia could answer, he was inside, fixing a loose shutter on the porch as if the place belonged to him.

Ray worked fast but sloppy—nails bent sideways, wood splitting like a bad metaphor for mercy. All the while he talked—about prison years in Parchman where he'd learned to pray louder than the men who wanted to kill him, about surviving winters in the Delta with nothing but a blanket and a pocketknife, about how God himself rode shotgun with him the day a guard dog clamped on his arm and wouldn't let go. His stories came out in a torrent, half-truth, half-parable, the line between them always blurred.

Claudia listened, sorting papers into neat piles that felt meaningless.

Part of her bristled at him being there—this stranger in a sarong, sweating bourbon and bravado, dragging his chaos into her grief. Red flags sprouted everywhere: the wink he threw her like they shared a secret, the way he leaned too close over the boxes, the strays lingering at the end of the drive as if waiting for his blessing.

Caroline, meanwhile, kept her arms crossed, eyes narrowing with every bent nail.

"You call that help?" She muttered, low enough for Claudia but not for Ray. "Looks like sabotage dressed up as charity."

But there was something else in him too—a rawness Claudia couldn't name, a kind of cracked-open truth she hadn't heard from anyone since their parents died. Where everyone else spoke in condolences and polite half-sentences, Ray spoke like fire, unfiltered, unashamed. Authentic, maybe. Or just ruin waiting to happen.

She caught herself laughing at one of his prison stories, shaking her head as if to warn herself. "You're either the biggest liar I've ever met," she said, "or the most honest man in Jackson County."

Ray grinned, teeth like broken piano keys. "Baby, I'm both."

And Claudia, against her better judgment—and over Caroline's steady protests—let him stay.

Five
MOONLIGHT

Margaret Ann Whitfield's invitation arrived on cream-embossed stationery. In Ocean Springs, Margaret Ann was the reigning 'goula widow—pearls stacked high, hair teased into a silver crown.

She had outlived three husbands, four hurricanes, and a lawsuit over rip rap erosion along the Pascagoula River. Folks still whispered she might have had a hand in two of those deaths, gossip that clung like Chanel No. 5.

Hosting luncheons was her sacrament.

The table stretched beneath a chandelier that flickered like it might short out, set with white linen and Waterford crystal she swore she'd bought in Mobile in '78. Claudia found herself squeezed between Chuck Langley, the town dentist and part-time Baptist deacon, and Haley McKinnon, who, with her husband Trevor, flipped coastal properties like gamblers at a blackjack table.

Conversation turned to Ray almost immediately.

"Such a man redeemed," Margaret Ann said, dabbing her lips. "After what he's been through, to come out and start a ministry that matters—it's practically Biblical."

Chuck Langley nodded. "I've seen the way he counsels folks outside my office. He's got a gift."

Haley leaned in, all mascara and ambition. "We're thinking about bringing him to our church outreach. Trevor says he's got presence—people just listen when he speaks."

Trevor smirked. "Presence pays. You can't buy authenticity. They don't fact-check redemption."

Haley laughed. Claudia caught something brittle beneath the polish.

Chuck smirked, then lowered his voice like a conspirator. "Truth is, if he weren't out there wrangling those drifters, they'd be camping behind my office. Police can only do so much. A man like Ray keeps the tide from coming in."

Margaret Ann sighed, folding her napkin as though in prayer. "He gives those poor souls dignity. And he gives us peace of mind. A win-win, if you ask me."

Claudia sipped her wine, feeling the edge of it. Ray wasn't just tolerated; he was canonized by cocktail hour—polished into legitimacy by Waterford crystal and Sunday best. He was their shield against the parts of the coast they didn't want to see.

Beneath her napkin, Claudia's thumb brushed a slip of paper tucked beside her place setting—a crumpled gas-station receipt with _Bayou Brotherhood_ scrawled in Ray's messy hand.

Margaret Ann caught her glance and smiled, too sweetly. "We all like to keep track of where our gifts go," she said, as if Claudia had asked.

Claudia slid the receipt into her purse, heart ticking faster. If it was meant as proof, or as bait, she couldn't tell. Either way, it was hers now.

The Gulf Coast had its own economy, older than casinos or shrimping, older than oil and paper mills: *guilt*.

Families rich since Reconstruction carried their money like perfume and their sins like shadows. They sat on museum boards, preservation societies, or garden clubs and called it virtue.

Reputation was their currency. They never admitted the source—slave timber, segregated shipyards, casinos that skimmed poor pockets dry.

Homelessness was to be kept at bay. Better to fund a faith-based program in some storefront than talk about housing policy.

Men like Brother Ray thrived on this system—charismatic, unqualified, broken enough to look authentic. He preached survival and repentance to the homeless, then sold redemption to the rich. His ministry was a revolving door of bologna sandwiches and revival songs, a sideshow of suffering that played well in donor reports. The poor were props; the rich were absolved.

Elites loved him because he cost them nothing. A check to Ray's Bayou Brotherhood Ministry meant you could sip cocktails on the yacht-club deck and talk about "the good work being done." It was outsourcing conscience—redemption by proxy. Cheap grace, bought as easily as lipstick at the Dollar General.

The irony never escaped Claudia: her parents had been Yacht Club people too, but the kind who showed up with casseroles, not checkbooks. Their wealth wasn't in reputation but in presence. Yet here sat the heirs of Pascagoula, laundering their power through people like Ray, a prophet in a sarong.

She'd always been drawn to men with sharp edges.

Her first boyfriend stole his uncle's truck and nearly ran them into a ditch on Highway 57, laughing while she clutched the dash. There was the one who swung at her after too much whiskey, and the one who swore he'd clean up but pawned her grandmother's ring instead.

It wasn't love she chased but voltage—the jolt of living on a fault line.

Her phone buzzed on the table.

A text from Ray, no punctuation, no explanation: meet me at the beach.

Caroline frowned. "If that's him, you don't answer," she said. "You've buried enough bad decisions."

Claudia slipped the phone into her purse, pretending not to hear, though the warning burned hotter than the wine in her throat.

• • •

At twilight, Front Beach was its own cathedral—blackwater sliding past cypress knees, the air thick with salt and pine. The surface caught the last bruise of daylight, broken by mullet jumping and the slow drift of herons returning to roost.

Claudia parked beneath the bridge and followed the sandy bank, the hum of cicadas rattling in her ears. This was the same bayou where her father had taught her to swim, where her mother's laughter once carried across the dock.

Now it was Ray's pulpit.

He was waist-deep, sarong floating around him, arms spread wide as if baptizing himself.

"C'mon, queen," he called. "Water's holy tonight."

She stepped in—cold against her skin. The air smelled of salt and magnolia.

She surfaced and watched him tread water with easy confidence, tattoos shimmering under the moonlight. For a moment she let herself drift, caught between memory and desire, knowing full well the red flags were already waving.

Claudia kicked off her sandals and stepped into the shallows. She hesitated by the shoreline, toes sinking into wet sand, and thought of her mother—running from her father's belt straight into a worse trap.

What terrified her wasn't Ray, but how easily she recognized the pull. She was her mother's daughter.

The water was warm, alive against her skin, carrying silt and memory in equal measure. Her father's voice surfaced first, instructing her how to hold her breath, how to let the water sit heavy on her chest without panic. She had been fearless even as a girl, swimming past docks with her lungs burning, daring herself deeper. Alligators never scared her; she believed they kept their distance from anyone who swam with confidence.

Her mother's laughter echoed next, drifting across the years. She saw her again on the dock with a plate of fried chicken in one hand and a towel in the other, making sure every child had food, every neighbor had drink, the social tide never running dry.

They were ghosts now, but the bayou remembered.

Moonlight broke free of the clouds, silvering the water. Claudia dove under, eyes open to the dark, feeling the familiar thrill of being suspended between fear and freedom.

When she surfaced, Ray was there, grinning like a prophet who'd called her to his altar.

And she laughed—because she had always loved erasing everything here.

Claudia surfaced, gasping. The present slammed back: Ray treading beside her, his tattooed shoulders gleaming under the moonlight. He grinned, the jagged ruins of his teeth catching the dim light.

Somewhere on the shore, Caroline's voice echoed in Claudia's mind—_Don't you dare bring another fire ant into this house._

Ray splashed water in her face, and she laughed too, the sound breaking loose like it belonged to someone else.

For a heartbeat it felt reckless and free.

She couldn't tell if she was laughing with him, at him, or at herself—only that she couldn't stop.

Six
THUMPS AND SLAPS

They left Ocean Springs before noon, windows down, Highway 90 sliding. Ray rode shotgun in a sarong the color of cantaloupe and scuffed cowboy boots, one heel chewed by a dog. He sang along to whatever the radio threw at him—Zydeco, Creedence, a Spanish preacher—and told Claudia the Atchafalaya was God's backbone and New Orleans balanced at the end.

By the time the skyline rose, the car had varnished with heat. They parked off Decatur and entered the Quarter: beaded balconies, bachelor parties in matching T-shirts, a brass band blasting "St. James Infirmary." Bourbon Street stank of sugar, spilled beer, and something animal.

Ray slipped through—high-fiving a bouncer, kissing air beside an old barmaid's cheek, tipping a kid spraying down the sidewalk. They ducked into a jazz dive where the piano sounded like it had been rolled down the stairs. Claudia let a Sazerac soften her edges; Ray knocked back a beer and a shot, spinning a story about the prison chaplain who smuggled him a harmonica "so I could remember air has a voice."

In Jackson Square, a tarot reader laid down The Tower, The Fool, The Star. "You're walking a rope, baby," she told Claudia. "But you always were a flyer."

Ray leaned back. "See? Prophecy."

Claudia rolled her eyes, but the idea lodged.

A teenage boy collapsed near the streetcar stop, limbs jerking against the pavement. The crowd pulled back.

Ray was already on his knees. "Easy, little brother," he said, sliding the kid onto his side, tucking the hem of his sarong under the boy's skull.

From his pocket came a battered card—emergency numbers scribbled in ink, "In Case of Emergency" across the top—and a Narcan vial taped to the back.

"Hold his shoulders," he told the friend. "Call him by name. Keep him here."

He sprayed both nostrils, his voice steady over the sirens rising in the distance. "Not today. Not on my watch."

The boy bucked, then sagged, breath catching.

EMTs arrived with a stretcher. Ray rattled off symptoms, timing, dosage, then stepped back, knees speckled with blood.

The crowd exhaled. Ray brushed it off.

"Carry on," he murmured, and to Claudia as they drifted away, "Sometimes the Lord gives you one you can actually fix."

He pocketed the Narcan refill the EMT slipped him "for the ministry," eyes already scanning for recruits.

She'd seen him grift, sermonize, swallow attention; she hadn't seen this. Competence. Why should saving a stranger make her want him more?

Over red beans and rice at a Formica counter, she decided Ray deserved backing. Later that week she wired a few hundred for "the ministry." Then gas money. A motel room. A printer. Each transfer small enough to excuse, large enough to matter.

She swore Caroline would never hear a word.

Nights at Bayou House. Porch light low. Whiskey sweating in jelly jars. Ghost stories that began as jokes and ended with someone staring at the treeline.

Ray stood on the steps, bending scripture around his biography. Strays hovered at the edges, close enough for warmth, far enough for escape.

Claudia told him about New York: boardrooms, pretending to care about things already decided, the view from forty-three floors that made the city look like a model.

Ray listened. When he spoke, it was about tents hidden from cops, which churches gave fresh socks, how to disarm a man mid-withdrawal. Volatile, yes. But useful.

One evening she and Ray floated in Fort Bayou. Cypress knees rose; mullet snapped the surface; bats crossed the air.

Headlights cut the pines. A Crown Vic parked crooked in the sand. Henri Toussaint climbed out, hat brim shading his eyes, and Yvette followed, denim skirt brushing her knees, towel slung over her shoulder.

"Well, look at God's timing," Ray called. "Y'all come to church?"

Henri tipped his hat. Yvette's mouth softened. "Evening, Claudia," she said.

They lingered at the waterline, swapping weather and names, the shorthand of people who had once shared a hallway.

Frankie's neon marlin buzzed. Inside, shrimp grease and bleach and secrets thickened the air. They took a corner table: Claudia and Yvette on the bench, Henri and Ray opposite. The jukebox believed in Otis Redding.

Ray ran hot until the bartender slid him a second whiskey on the house. Then he slapped the bar, announced he was "gonna drain the Jordan," and vanished.

Silence dropped.

Yvette leaned toward Claudia. "You were a flyer even back then."

Claudia smiled. "Some habits don't die."

"Some habits hunt," Yvette said. "We've seen him. He gathers the hungry, the hurt. Sometimes he feeds them. Sometimes he feeds on them."

Henri's gaze didn't lift. "He shines. And shining's a kind of lure."

Yvette covered Claudia's hand. "But the trickster shines brightest before he steals everything. Lock your doors."

"I'll keep my pockets zipped," Claudia said.

The bathroom door banged open. Ray reemerged, radiant. "To the work," he said. "To the ministry."

Claudia lifted her glass.

The weeks that followed blurred.

Then came the drum circle. It started as a joke—Ray calling it "Sunday service for sinners"—but it grew. Every Friday they hauled driftwood and candles to the beach, joined by hippies and heretics: ex-bartenders, barefoot retirees, women who sold crystals out of their trunks.

Someone always brought a conga, someone else a tambourine. Ray found a cajón at a thrift store, polished it with cooking oil, beating out rhythms that slid from bass thumps to slaps.

They'd play until their hands blistered. Claudia sat in the sand, bottle between her knees, watching firelight on faces that had run from too much.

For a while, they were happy—not perfect, not stable.

Sunday mornings smelled like pancakes on a camp stove, syrup stolen from the Waffle House. Sometimes they drove nowhere—asphalt, salt air, wind through holes in the truck's cab.

She told herself this was what peace might look like: pretending it could last.

Seven

GASLIGHT

By morning the yard at Bayou House looked like a carnival. Two tents sagged under the live oak, a blue tarp strung with extension cords that ran nowhere. Beer cans in the monkey grass. Someone had used a Folgers can for an ashtray. A Bible lay face down in the dew, pages bloated, underlined in yellow. A pill bottle lay in the hydrangeas—another man's name on the label. The scent was sweat, malt liquor, and woodsmoke.

Ray called it "temporary sanctuary."

"They just need a soft landing, queen," he said, shouldering past her with a crate of canned beans and a fifth of Evan Williams under the top layer.

At dusk he led a prayer circle by the fire barrel, Bluetooth speaker playing old gospel. His followers swayed, a few wept on cue, one nodded off mid-amen. Afterward they flooded the porch, hungry and grateful and loud, and Claudia handed out bologna sandwiches because her hands needed a job.

In the kitchen she counted cups and plates, the pulse climbing when she saw the pill bottle again beside the sink. Yvette's warning replayed—lock your doors—and she wondered if she'd already misplaced them.

Ray's asks started small. Gas money. A motel room for a woman "too spun out for the yard." A printer cartridge. He made it sound like logistics, tasks only she was competent enough to complete.

"You're the one with structure," he said. "I'm the fire. We make a church."

When she hesitated, he shrugged. "Or don't. I'll take care of it. Somehow."

She handed him a card "for a couple hours." Later that night he tucked both her bank cards into his wallet "so we don't lose track with all the moving parts," and she didn't correct the we.

Complaints came: a neighbor at the fence line, arms crossed, asking how long the camp out would last; a police cruiser rolling by slow, then slower the next night. Caroline left a message Claudia didn't finish. Margaret Ann texted a prayer-hands emoji and "Stay strong—this work offends the small-minded." Henri and Yvette sent no message, but Claudia caught sight of them at the Piggly Wiggly—Henri tipping his hat, Yvette looking through her.

By the third week, her bank app showed the damage. ATM withdrawals labeled OCEAN SPRINGS MART. A charge at a pawn shop in Gautier. Two Cash App transfers to BayouBrotherhoodMinistries that hadn't existed yesterday. Claudia scrolled.

She found him on the porch.

"Ray," she said. "Where are my cards."

He blinked innocence. "In the lock-box. Safe."

"What lock-box."

"The lock-box of faith," he said, then laughed when she didn't. "Kitchen drawer, top right."

She opened it. Old menus. A corkscrew. No lock-box. No cards.

"Hey now," he said, standing close. "Let's not do this rich-lady dance. You told me to float the ministry. You cried about wanting meaning and here it is. We're building community."

"I didn't authorize a pawn shop."

He spread his hands. "We sold the busted generator for cash because the boys needed meds. Your meds, if you want to be literal, because these are your people now."

"You took out six hundred in cash."

"Your memory's off since your folks passed," he said. "You handed me that cash in the kitchen after yoga, said 'make it move.' I said 'are you sure' and you said 'I'm done counting.' You don't remember because you've been dissociating. Trauma, baby. I learned that word from Lila."

She looked at the app again.

"Put the cards on the table."

He shook his head. "Why are you controlling me? You think because I wear a dress and not a tie you get to parent me? That's colonizer energy, Claudia. You're turning into the very boardroom boys you said you hated."

"Stop." Her voice cracked. "Stop making me the problem."

He kissed her forehead. "I love you for your heart," he whispered. "Don't let the devil make you count it. We got people in the yard who'd be dead without us. You want me to tell them Mama had a panic and cut off the food?"

She closed her eyes.

That night the yard had a bonfire and a fight. Two of his followers argued over a backpack, punches swung, someone went down, then up again. Ray waded between them shouting "peace, peace."

After, he found Claudia in the hallway with the door half shut.

"See?" He said. "Family. Messy. Worth it."

She slept badly and woke to a rooster that didn't live here. The tents had multiplied by two. Someone had dragged a couch onto the grass. The couch had opinions about rain.

When Claudia stepped outside, Yvette's words flickered again: the trickster shines brightest before he steals everything.

Claudia changed her bank password at noon. She texted Ray that she needed her cards back to "reconcile expenses." Two minutes later he was at the door with the smile that sold kingdoms. He handed them over dramatically, palms up.

"Never say I don't trust you," he said. "We're partners."

By evening the cards were missing again.

"How," she said.

"You left them out on the counter," he said, already hurt. "Anybody could have grabbed them. I told you we needed a system and you insisted on control. Do you see how your fear invites chaos? You make the hole; I patch it. And then you punish me for patching."

She felt something tilt. Henri's voice in memory: he shines, and shining's a kind of lure.

On the third night of the week, a follower she didn't recognize knocked to use the shower. Then another asked for "the good towels." On the fourth, a woman vomited in the azaleas and cried for a son who might exist. On the fifth, Ray gathered them all and preached a tenderness that made Claudia want to believe again.

He called her Sister Claudia from the porch and thanked her for "holding the gate." The yard murmured amen.

She stood in the kitchen with a sponge and a ledger she'd stopped updating.

"You're imagining things," he told her.

She repeated it.

Eight
SLIPPING AND FALLING

By noon the tents had multiplied. The couch on the lawn had gone soft with mildew. Beer cans sat in the monkey grass. The yard had turned into festival detritus—glow sticks braided into ponytails, a Bluetooth speaker thumping country–EDM remixes, a hula hoop flashing. Skunky weed drifted under the oaks; something harder hung in it. An Altoids tin of paper tabs and smiley-face pressies passed palm to palm. Somebody spray painted a plywood "ART" sign and propped it against the fire barrel.

Claudia counted what could be counted—plates, towels, the way her bank balance kept thinning. When she bent to pick up a can, the receipt in her pocket crinkled.

She found Ray in the kitchen lining up paper cups.

"It's over," she said. "The camp goes. My cards stay with me. We're done playing church."

He didn't look up. "We don't play church, queen. We are church."

"You took eight hundred cash in two days and pawned my generator."

"For insulin. For food." He smiled. "You always want to talk about money when we're saving lives. That's colonizer math."

"No more," she said, reaching past him for the drawer. "Give me my cards."

He closed the drawer with his hip and turned. From the pocket of his sarong, the corner of a debit card flashed.

"After everything," he said. "After I lifted you out of your grief and gave you family."

"You stole," she said.

The shove was simple. A block to the shoulder that found its angle.

She went backward into the doorjamb and heard the pop before she felt it, then hot white.

The air narrowed. Her stomach turned metallic.

The pain arrived, bright and specific, from wrist to elbow.

Ray was already there, hands fluttering. "Baby girl—no, no, no—I didn't—I barely touched—why'd you lean like that?"

Tears came easy for him; they always had.

He reached for her, then away, then for her again. "I'm sorry, I'm sorry, you drove me to it, you know how you get—counting till the devil gets in your head."

She slid to the floor.

He wrapped a dish towel around the forearm and kissed her hair. "Shh. Shh. It's a sprain. You're dramatic."

"Let me fix it. I'll fix it." He lifted the towel; the card was gone.

She should have gone to the ER. Instead she let him tape her with athletic wrap.

He gave her ibuprofen and poured whiskey to chase it and told them in the yard to keep it down because "Mama's resting." By evening he was preaching from the porch again, and she was in the back bedroom staring at the ceiling fan.

By morning there was a wall between what happened and what could be told.

She texted Caroline: tripped over the stupid couch, lol. Sprained my wrist. She told the neighbor at the fence she'd "tweaked something" moving boxes. She told herself it would be fine by Friday.

It wasn't. The wrist swelled.

She learned to cradle it, to keep the hand below her heart, to smile past the throb. She practiced sentences that did not include the word shove.

At Frankie's that night, the bar light was low.

Frankie took one look at the way she held herself and set a glass down without asking, then didn't move away. "What happened," she said.

"Slipped on the back steps," Claudia said. "The rain."

Dottie arrived. "That man," she said, and didn't finish.

Caroline arrived with an ice pack. "You're guarding it," she said. "Let me see."

"I'm fine," Claudia said. "Really."

Lila hovered at the edge of the group, hands braided in front of her. "We don't know what happened," she said carefully. "Let's not project."

Ray breezed in, kissed the air near Claudia's temple, grabbed a stool, ordered a round "for the saints at the table."

The room accommodated him: shoulders eased, eyes drifted.

Claudia watched and thought, he shines, and shining's a kind of lure.

Henri and Yvette were there. They took the end of the booth without asking.

"We'll set lights for you," Yvette said. "Tie a red string to the leg of your bed. Put a bowl of water under it to catch what falls off him when he sleeps. Salt the thresholds. Pepper, too—he won't cross pepper if he's meaning you harm. My grandma taught me tricks you can do with a broom."

"And photocopy your cards and license tonight," she said. "Put the copies in my glove box. If he empties your wallet, you'll still have a name."

Henri's voice was low. "The work is the work. And sometimes the work is leaving." He slid a napkin across: a mechanic's number, a storage unit on Live Oak, a note—spare lock paid—in his hand.

"It was—stupid. Me. I slipped."

Yvette didn't argue. She squeezed. "We were girls together," she said. "We learned to lie to keep the grown-ups comfortable."

Ray returned. "What'd I miss, my prophets?" He clapped. "Game time—who's got a testimony?"

"Not tonight," Frankie said.

He laughed.

He raised his glass. "To grace," he said. "To the work."

Claudia lifted hers with the left hand and felt the right fail.

She slid the receipt from her pocket under the napkin and pressed her palm on it. She drank.

Outside, rain started. When Ray's laugh rose over the room, Claudia didn't join. She counted the exits.

Nine
MAMA GHOST

The house breathed around Claudia, giving back every soft step as a complaint. She drifted room to room with her right arm cradled against her ribs, the wrap dingy from overuse, the bone a live wire whenever she forgot and reached.

Outside, the yard lay quiet. Ray's voice rose and fell. Inside, dust spun in the window light.

She opened a hall closet: picnic baskets, tangled Christmas lights, a hatbox. Beneath it, the blue Rubbermaid with the photos—heavy when you only have one good hand. She nudged it to the rug with her foot, sat cross-legged, and lifted the lid. The receipt fell out with it. She shoved it in her pocket.

Her father first: hospital scrubs starched, stethoscope, his face creased in that tired way good doctors get when they've learned how to be gentle without lying.

In one shot he stood under a "Singing River" sign, squinting into winter light; in another he laughed with a nurse at a station that hadn't changed since 1989. He wasn't a believer—had said so in the night she was twelve and asked what happened after—but he believed in showing up.

Caroline's voice, half-teasing, had once labeled him "Saint Practical," a man who preached by staying late on call.

Her mother in a sundress at a town fish fry, hair caught in wind, a metal spatula raised. The long tables sagged under bowls—slaw, potato salad, hush puppies—coolers open. In every frame she was mid-laughter, head thrown back, drink in one hand, on someone's shoulder. A woman who'd converted for a marriage and rejected the pious along the way.

They'd called themselves atheists in the same tone other couples used for "Methodist" or "Lutheran"—not as a dare, simply as coordinates. Near the end, he hedged with Pascal's wager and sat straighter in the pew; near the end, she hummed loud enough to drown the sermon. Neither would've trusted a man whose gospel needed a spotlight. Both believed a casserole at the right time could change the world. Caroline had inherited that instinct, showing up with gumbo pots and cornbread for every crisis. Claudia wondered what Caroline would bring to this crisis—if she could name it without choking on the shame.

Claudia felt the house tilt to that truth and then tilt back. She let her mother's photos spread like tarot cards at a reading. From the kitchen window, the bayou showed itself in a thin slice, dark and patient, the color of secrets.

Her mother's voice arrived. "Don't let a man steal your fire, Claudia."

"I didn't," she whispered, an answer that convinced no one. Her hand brushed the receipt in her pocket.

At the bottom of the Rubbermaid sat the small cedar box with a Ziploc of ashes double-bagged. Claudia lifted it, thumb rubbing the lid.

The promise: the Viking funeral on Fort Bayou they'd laughed about and then written down, her mother delighted by the drama of a flaming boat. They'd talked skiff sizes and permits and how far from the pier you needed to push. They'd argued cedar vs. pine, candles vs. lamp oil, hymns vs. silence. Her mother wanted Otis Redding. Her father voted for quiet. In the end they'd settled on fire, night, and secrecy—a ceremony small enough for three.

Then hospitals, funerals, the ministry blooming in her yard like tree fungus. Every week she meant to do it, and every week something intervened: a fight by the fire barrel, a follower needing the spare room, Ray calling her "Sister Claudia" from the porch. The skiff she'd marked for the send-off ended up hauling ice and a generator to a "revival," then vanished to somebody's uncle, pawned or promised, no one could say. Caroline had texted twice that week asking if she'd followed through; Claudia lied both times.

Guilt worked whenever she passed the boathouse, whenever she saw lamp oil in a hardware aisle, whenever the bayou wore its moonlight and dared her.

She set the cedar box on the dining table and went looking for candles. The junk drawer coughed up tea lights, a taper stub, matches from Frankie's bar. She started to line them up, then stopped—too church. Instead she poured a ring of kosher salt onto the tabletop and scratched a vegvísir—the Norse wayfinder, Viking cousin to a Haitian vevè, a pentagram, more compass than conjure. She set eight tea lights at its points and the taper in the center.

She struck a match, hesitated, and laughed at herself.

"Tomorrow," she said. "Tomorrow night, Mama. I'll do it right."

Don't let a man steal your fire, the voice said again,

Ray's laugh carried in from the yard. The plumbing sighed—a low, wet groan. The air was thick with bleach and rain rot.

In the yard someone whooped; glass popped like a small knuckle cracking. A Bluetooth speaker hiccuped gospel and then fell back into country. Claudia put her good hand flat on the cedar lid and felt the very faint rattle of the house through the wood, the way all structures hum when you ask more of them than they were built to hold.

The light outside shifted—late afternoon into that hour the Coast does so well, where everything goes honeyed before it goes black. She set a single tea light burning, not a ceremony, just a pinprick to mark intention. The flame trembled.

Her phone buzzed and buzzed and stopped. She didn't get it. She sat with her mother's photographs. She slid the cedar box back into the Rubbermaid and left it near the door. Tonight she would sleep.

Outside, a breeze stirred the live oaks and set the leaves whispering. The receipt pressed against her thigh.

Ten
SHAKEDOWN

The corner store at Porter and Government—fluorescents buzzing, cooler motors grinding, the air a mix of fryer oil, Pine-Sol, and cigarettes. Claudia cradled her arm against her ribs and moved slowly. Milk. Bread. Ibuprofen. She held a basket firmly with her good arm; appearing fine had become a reflex. She hadn't come here for the prices. She'd come because it was a place where Ray's people didn't bother her. Until now.

A bell chimed and a boy in light-up sneakers tugged his mother toward the freezer case. "Popsicle," he whispered. The woman—thin, tired, her sweatshirt sliding off one shoulder—counted coins in her palm. "Maybe next time, baby." She put a half-gallon of milk in her basket, added a loaf of white bread, ramen bricks, a bruised apple. The name tag on her chest read SANDRA. The boy pressed his face to the glass.

The door banged. Ray breezed in with two of his followers, laughter ahead of them. He wore a sun-faded sundress and chewed-up cowboy boots, a ministry lanyard hanging from his neck.

"Afternoon, saints," he started. He rapped the counter and winked at the clerk. "Blessings on your enterprise, brother."

The clerk—skin sallow under the lights—nodded and kept scanning. A laminated sign was taped to the glass: NO CREDIT. NO TABS. NO EXCEPTIONS.

Ray ignored it. Claudia had seen him do versions of this before. Usually smaller. Usually with a smile that made people call it help. He moved toward Sandra's aisle, plucked a rotisserie chicken from the heated case and inhaled. "Glory," he said. To his boys: "Grab what we came for."

They moved with practiced ease. One swept chips, jerky, and Gatorade into a basket. The other opened the freezer and handed a popsicle to the boy without asking. The kid blinked, then bit. Blue syrup striped his chin; the wooden stick printed his palm.

"We're the Bayou Brotherhood Ministry," Ray announced. "Feeding the flock today." He snagged diapers from the end-cap, set them down. "Put these on our account, partner. God keeps a ledger."

The clerk's mouth tightened. "There's no account." He didn't look at Ray when he said it. He looked at the camera in the corner and pointed at the sign. "No tabs."

Ray smiled. "We've always settled up right, haven't we? Ask around." He tapped the counter. "Don't be hard-hearted. We got babies outside, ain't any of them mine."

Claudia watched the room. The man in the fishing shirt pretended to need sunglasses. A woman in scrubs studied the gum rack. Nobody broke it.

Sandra stepped into the space at the counter, coins in her hand. "Can I—" she started, then stopped when Ray pivoted.

"Let me bless you, sister," he said, taking the milk and bread from her. He nudged her items onto the counter with theirs. "We're all together here." To the boy: "You like that pop?

That's the Lord saying yes."

The clerk scanned. Sandra held out a few dollars. The clerk took them, made change, and set it on the glass.

Ray covered the change with his hand and took it. "We'll steward this for you," he said gently. "Keep the devil out your budget."

He added the rotisserie chicken to Sandra's bag. "Now you can eat like queens."

"Hey," the clerk said. "That's her change."

Ray leaned on the glass. "We're taking care of her. The ministry's got it. Don't make this ugly." Claudia saw the clerk's throat work.

Sandra swallowed, eyes on her son's shoes. "It's okay," she murmured. "Thank you."

Ray turned up the charm for the store. "Community," he said, patting the diapers. "This is how it's supposed to work." He lifted the chicken like an offering and passed the bag to Sandra. "You're with us now."

Claudia felt her stomach flip. She watched Ray spend the word ministry, watched him expand, watched Sandra shrink. Milk, bread, chicken, change—not enough to call the police on.

And there she stood, silent.

The clerk glanced at Claudia. Her good hand tightened on the basket handle until her knuckles went pale. She could feel her voice in her chest and still couldn't push it out.

The instinct—to smooth, to stand down—rose. Yvette said shine is a lure, and her mother said don't let a man steal your fire, and Ray said we're building community.

The woman in scrubs finally stepped forward and put a dollar on the counter, then another. "For the kid," she said without looking at anyone. Her badge read LPN. The clerk slid the bills toward the register as if that made them official.

Ray clapped. "That's the spirit," he said. "See? The body of Christ—functioning." He reached into the charity jar by the cigarettes—loose change for a softball team—and swirled it with his fingers, coins chiming, then left it where it was, a mercy disguised as restraint. The jar wobbled; the clerk steadied it with two fingertips, then wiped the glass where Ray's touch had smudged a crescent.

They moved to the door. Ray spotted Claudia and grinned. "There she is," he said. "Sister Claudia, keeper of the gate." He kissed the air near her cheek.

"You took her change," she said.

He laughed as if they were flirting. "You saw me redistribute it. Baby, that's ministry." His smile held a second longer than it needed to.

Outside, the heat hit. The boy licked blue from his knuckles. Sandra shouldered the bag, gave Claudia a quick look and crossed the lot. Ray and his boys peeled toward the alley, tearing open the jerky before the door swung shut. Blue drops spattered the concrete.

The clerk took a rag, sprayed the counter, and wiped in slow circles.

Claudia set her basket down and stepped outside. She leaned against the stucco, her breath shallow. Authenticity had always been her defense of him. But there was nothing honest in what she'd just watched.

Across the street, a neon church sign flickered: LET US NOT LOVE WITH WORDS OR SPEECH BUT WITH ACTIONS. She laughed once, slid to the ground in the shade, forearm tucked to her stomach, forehead against the wall.

She went back in and told the clerk she was sorry.

"For what?" He asked, polite, baffled.

Mumbling, she shrugged and left. On the sidewalk, she snapped the popsicle stick the boy had dropped and put it in the trash. She didn't know what came next. She only knew she couldn't say his name the same way again.

Eleven
HARBOR OAKS

Sirens. Blue light ran across the white columns of Harbor Oaks. The guard shack gate was stuck open, a patrol unit nosed crosswise; neighbors in robes clustered behind sawhorses.

Claudia parked at the boat launch and walked in, her arm strapped close to her ribs. For a heartbeat she saw it all wrong—Caroline on the porch swing, one leg tucked under her. Yellow tape and the scent of ozone.

Her body caught up to her eyes a second late. The air was sour—salt, creosote, and algae. She could smell bleach before she saw any. She thought again of the corner store and wished she had spoken sooner. Caroline appeared beside her, hair pulled back, sweatshirt zipped to her chin.

Claudia looked at her sister: "We don't need to jump to conclusions."

"Back behind the tape, ladies," a deputy said.

Beyond the yellow line: Haley and Trevor McKinnon's house, four stories on stilts under strobe light. A crime scene tech in paper booties walked out holding a Ziploc with a coil of gray cord and something white at the end that looked like a bone. Another tech followed, palming a handset like a relic.

"02:04," a detective's voice dictated. "Phone dead at the NID. RJ11 cut clean."

Neighbors were busy having theories. "Break-in," a man in a Saints hoodie declared to his wife, as if naming it helped. "Kids again." She shook her head and whispered about seeing a white sedan at 1 a.m.

with no headlights. The guard jotted in a notebook that had already sweated through at the corners.

Claudia didn't ask anything. She looked where the cops looked: the hedgerow where someone had crawled, the side gate bowed at the latch, the dark rectangle of a window with a spider-webbed crack low enough to be deliberate. She tried not to imagine the sound that went with that fracture.

"02:07," another timestamp: "Two tight groups. Subsonic. No one heard a thing."

"02:08. Caliber small. Twenty-two most likely. Oil filter trick."

Another bag came past, heavy with a small door in it. "Safe interior," the label read. Someone asked for "the inventory list" and got told there wasn't one yet. Someone else said, "Ledger's not here." The word ledger stuck.

Caroline leaned in: "Ledger?" Her voice was flat, sharp. Claudia shook her head, already retreating into silence.

She angled for more air and found the mailbox instead, open-mouthed with a smiley-face magnet. A gloved hand reached in and came back with a cheap flip phone in a quart bag, battery popped, screen dark as a shut eye. The officer held it up for a camera flash that made the street howl blue-white for a breath.

"02:11. Flip phone recovered, prepaid. Battery separated." Radio chatter scratched around them. "Be advised, Shell station on Washington has footage—male, cowboy boots, plaid jacket, bought an oil filter and duct tape at zero-zero-twenty-seven. Sending unit."

Cowboy boots.

Caroline's eyes found hers. Claudia's mouth stayed shut—again.

A woman in a robe began to cry softly without visible motion. A man said "Jesus" like a password, then said it again as if the second time might open a door. The guard's phone buzzed and buzzed and he looked at it and didn't answer.

"Ma'am," the young deputy said again, more duty than warning, and Claudia stepped back a half-shoe into the safe world where law was still pretending to be a fence.

She didn't know Haley and Trevor like she knew their kind: the subdivision laugh, the tan everybody agreed with, the escrow magic trick at closing. She thought of Margaret Ann's white linen tablecloths and Pastor Reese's smooth hands, and felt her stomach roll the way boats do when a wake arrives from the wrong angle.

A detective in an untucked oxford leaned over the hood of a cruiser and wrote slower than the night wanted. "Who finds them," he asked the uniform beside him.

"07:02," the reply. "Housekeeper. Said she smelled bleach."

Bleach tries to be the last word. It never is. The bay held the sirens like a bowl, the sound sloshing. Somebody on the dock down the block dropped a net into the water, because habit doesn't check the news. Glass ticked somewhere as it cooled.

Claudia put her tongue to the back of her teeth and tasted battery. She didn't have a fact yet—only patterns repeating: a ledger missing, a burner in a mailbox, a man in boots at a gas station.

Don't let me be late again.

The tape made a footpath of light across the grass. A tech knelt and dropped the cut end of a phone line into a bag and turned the zip closed with an economy that belonged in surgery. The copper winked under the strobe like a nerve remembering pain.

"02:15. Log the stub. Seventeen-B."

She backed away, because staying would mean answering questions she wasn't ready to ask. She walked slowly back to her car as blue light skimmed the water.

• • •

At 8:12 a.m. the HOA's e-mail blast ricocheted across Pelican Point: gates rotating, codes changing, vendors to be kept at the curb. By noon the cul-de-sac was confused—gardeners stalled on sidewalks, delivery vans turning circles, neighbors forgetting which code went with which week. Everyone understood what the memo didn't say. Security was the word they used when they meant distance.

A tech in paper booties bagged and logged the evidence: the severed phone line, a prepaid flip with its battery popped in the mailbox, the safe door removed without marks. On the sill, a thin smear of oil caught the lab light; a swab, a cap, a number.

By nightfall police light raced across the water—red, blue, red strobes cutting the water. Two bodies went out under sheets.

Claudia watched them go and knew the night had already decided more than it was saying.

Twelve
SAVED

He showed up barefoot. Isaiah "Ice" Duvernay, thirty-four, Angola prison dust still pressed into his jeans. Ray hauled him onto the plywood stage behind the bait shop. "This is my brother Isaiah," Ray told the flock. "Fresh out the gates. God melted Ice today."

Ice tried to smile and didn't quite manage. A former spiderweb tattoo on his wrist now a rosary braid. His eyes did the math on exits. He told the microphone he'd found Jesus in a mop closet. The crowd said amen.

Claudia stood at the back, her bad arm tucked up. She clapped when the room clapped. Ray wrapped Ice in a hug and announced a love offering for the "new life." An orange bucket passed. Claudia dropped in a twenty. Protection, she told herself.

Later, by the fire barrel, Ray gave Ice boots—cowboy, scuffed, chewed at the heel. "Walk in victory," he said. Ice turned them over.

Without showmanship, Ice crouched at the barrel. He slid his hand in and pinched a coal like it was a marble, shifted it to the = side, and let it go. The sizzle was small. No flinch. No prayer. A black crescent burned into his palm.

Claudia's arm throbbed.

• • •

At Frankie's, the days after Harbor Oaks snapped into a pattern. They started tracking the money flow of Ray's ministry, trying to connect the dots. Frankie spread receipts across her back-office table: Cash App screenshots, ATM slips, a gas-station still.

"Phone hustle," she said. "Prison call tree. You ring soft-hearted folks, call it benevolence, skim it on the way through. Somebody skims too much; somebody gets mad."

Nobody said it aloud, but this wasn't academic. Dottie wheeled in a corkboard. Lila snapped a photo of the bare wall—"Before and after."

"Ain't a scrapbook," Frankie said, pinning the first sheet. "It's a fucking murder board."

Headers in black marker: MONEY / PHONES / CASINOS / CHURCH / BOOTS. Red string. Visitor logs, casino slips, benevolence minutes—tacked up. Frankie added a Shell still—cowboy boots, oil filter, duct tape. She slid a marlin matchbook into the corner.

"We're not solving who," Dottie said. "We're solving how to end him."

"Run him out," Frankie corrected. "Not a courtroom fantasy. Exile. Strip the donors, salt the ground, make him small enough to step over."

Claudia stared at the board. "I want him gone," she said. "He broke my arm and told me I made him do it. I want every person who wrote him a check to see what they bought."

"Good," Frankie said. "Receipts, not rumors. A ledger and a timeline. We cut his oxygen—money, cover, myth."

• • •

Bayou House the next morning: grill smoke, Bluetooth gospel, coolers sweating. Ray leaned close to Ice.

"They skimmed the Lord's money," Ray said. "Flips and chips. Wolves in realtor suits."

Ice stared at the water. Ray nudged the boots. "Shepherds handle wolves."

"Say when," Ice said.

Claudia, stacking coolers one-handed, caught the edges: McKinnons. Benevolence. Stolen.

At noon, cruisers rolled in. Deputies cuffed Ray for obstruction of justice. He crossed himself. His people started shouting obscenities. Ice stepped when Claudia did.

Booking room: cinder-block, hum. Ray gave alibis in hymns. The detective laid out timestamps: Shell at 12:27. Bridge at 12:54. Harbor Oaks at 1:43. Murder at 2:04. "Where you been, Ray?"

Ray smiled. "Time's fuzzy when the Spirit moves."

"Clocks aren't," the detective said.

• • •

Pastor Reese and Margaret Ann Whitfield bailed him out twenty-four hours later, cameras flashing. Statements covered Ice too— revival testimony, near passed out, the Spirit to blame.

Belief was the easiest currency to launder.

The new phone arrived on the third day. "A donor," Ray said. "Didn't want the ministry held back."

Frankie thumbed her call logs. "Numbers don't migrate overnight. That's a burner in church clothes."

The timeline: missing half hours, boots. Claudia shook Ray's sarong into the washer and a matchbook fell to the floor—oil stained.

She held it.

Ray appeared, kissed air near her face, called her queen.

She touched the matchbook in her apron.

Later that night, at Frankie's, the women laid out slips, logs, and minutes.

"We're not asking you to accuse," Frankie said. "We're asking you to notice."

"I'll notice," Claudia said. "I'll call if I see the ledger."

"Two hours is forever if you're planning," Frankie said.

Claudia wrote it on the whiteboard: Call Dottie. Find ledger.

Ice has killer hands. Ray aims them.

She capped the marker, and listened to Ray's new phone buzz while the old one lay silent.

Thirteen
POWERPOINT SAINTS

Against the back wall of Frankie's office, thumbtacks, PostIt notes, and red string formed a constellation on the corkboard. Frankie called it her gospel wall.

Start at Pastor Reese's Benevolence Fund—widows folding bills into envelopes to pay for medicine, utility bills, summer shoes. From there the ledger bent: Benevolence routed into Brotherhood accounts, Brotherhood siphoning out repeatable amounts—$9,980, always just below the threshold—into two casinos: Magnolia Crown and Sandbar Belle. Too small to trigger audits; Chips in, grace out.

On another pin: an escrow addendum from a McKinnon flip—line item BBM Consult Fee—circled, the word plumbing beside it.

Dottie fed the board. Angola visitor logs with Isaiah Duvernay's name. Parole paperwork with curfews and job checks. Late-night trips to casinos, slips matching Claudia's stolen generator, pawnshop tickets.

Meanwhile Pastor Reese ministry newsletter hit every mailbox in Ocean Springs—glossy stock, photos staged. On the cover Ray posed arm-in-arm with Reese, Bible in one hand, shovel in the other. Inside: ribbon-cuttings and generous grant language. If Reese got his way, Ray wouldn't stop at sermons; he'd slide into City Hall come fall—faith and commerce married on glossy card stock.

Where others saw authenticity, Claudia saw architecture. And she knew Ray was just a fixture installed by the system. She wrote it down: "Architecture, not authenticity."

Her assigned task—help wire the "community presentation" Reese wanted—sat on her laptop like bait. The deck gleamed where it needed to: bullet points about economic uplift, workforce development, youth engagement. Promises polished until they reflected light. But in her drafts folder one PowerPoint slide lived and would not make the public cut: COMMUNITY IMPACT—Bullets We Won't Admit.

As Claudia dug deeper, the shock came quietly, in the margins she never read aloud. The record didn't open with ceremonies or smiling photos beside checks. It opened with funerals—mothers keening beside coffins paid for with embezzled tithes, parolees running errands that ended in blood. A pipeline blessed in church and rinsed in casinos.

The pattern kept extending. It wasn't limited to one town or one preacher. In the seventies, bars paired with storefront churches to move jukebox money and dice cash under revival tents. By the nineties, the same structure carried polish—media ministries, seed-time promises wired before checks cleared. Court filings surfaced across Tennessee, Georgia, Florida: ministries operating as front doors for ledger fraud, preacher–developer partnerships folding land grabs into "community development."

After COVID, the structure widened. Relief loans folded into schemes run through sham nonprofits. Veterans' benefits rerouted through bogus seminaries. Food banks stripped from the inside. She read indictments out of Fort Lauderdale—ministers charged with tax and securities fraud—and case after case out of Georgia and Tennessee, each resolving into the same layout. Saints rendered in PowerPoint. Pulpits rising from shell companies.

She stacked the filings until the pile blurred. Churches registered as nonprofits while operating as laundromats. "Community partnerships" masking rezoning flips. Federal block grants and historic tax credits laundered through mayor's offices in sweetheart deals to developers. Traveling evangelists serving as envelopes, moving money from one mid-level operator to the next. Institutions that promised salvation had hardened into vaults nobody audited.

Pulpits were bank vaults. People tithed for groceries and light bills, never imagining those crumpled fives and tens landing on a contractor's invoice.

Frankie stood in the doorway. Dottie pulled receipts that smelled of paper and long nights. Lila traced the route of checks. And out on his shiny press pages, Pastor Reese lingered over Ray's name until the tune of it sounded like a ballot ask.

This was no longer rot—it was design. If Ray's ministry could be converted into political capital—donors funneled through Brotherhood accounts feeding campaigns; churches staging public works while land quietly changed hands—then the infection would spread through zoning, policing, and procurement. The rot would be zoned into permanence.

The betrayal was institutional. She wanted faith to be real—she needed something communal that wasn't transactional—but the receipts told another gospel: belief could be sold wholesale.

She drafted language that would never see the water cooler in the church basement. Lines that read like municipal policy but smelled of disclosure: transparency clauses, donor vetting, independent audits of benevolence accounts. Practical grace, enforceable mercy. In her private deck she planted the kind of architecture she trusted: accountable systems, not performative optics.

At night she thought of her parents. Their illnesses had been paid for by people who pledged and preached while dollars slid away. Her mother's Lewy-body confusion, her father's hospice—the bills that piled while sermons promised miracles—these were not spiritual tragedies but financial autopsies. She imagined pinning receipts to their mailboxes like last rites. There was fury in that visualization, precise as bookkeeping.

The work became less an investigation and more an act of excavation: pull the drywall, trace the pipes, map the flow. It was unromantic, but it was how cities and consciences were fixed. She kept thinking like someone who builds things: find the joints, follow the seams, expose the plumbing. If she could show how the water ran, she could shut the valves.

Claudia was finally ready to show the skeletal outlines of what she had found to Frankie, Dottie, and Lila.

"Here are the sewer lines," she said. "And now we've got the receipts."

Frankie nodded, studying Claudia's research. "We take the heart out of their bullshit," she said. "Make the money pipeline the problem, not the people."

In a town that worshipped appearances, Claudia still wanted to believe in the sacred. Instead, she was learning to believe in corrupt systems.

Pastor Reese's new newsletter was passed around all over town. Ray's face smiled from glossy pages that could be folded and mailed, faith pre-stamped for delivery. The plan to put him on the ballot felt close enough to smell: campaign flyers, donors courted with "moral leadership," city contracts tithed back as thanks.

Claudia dragged the slide deck into a folder, closed her laptop, and slipped a copy of the BBM invoice into Frankie's hand. She watched the women prepare to do what churches seldom allow: demand a ledger. If the pulpit had become a laundering device, their counter-sermon would be accounting. If institutions could betray, they could also be repaired—by new rules, not revelations.

It was not a neat plan. It was slow, legal, draining, but possibly holy. If not a flawed man like Ray, Claudia still wanted to believe in something. "I want faith that's not a funnel," she wrote in her journal.

Fourteen
THE TOUSSAINTS

Henry and Yvette Toussaint's place leaned toward the bay on a narrow spit of land just off Government Street, where Ocean Springs ran out of money and pavement. Spanish moss hung low from centuries-old live oaks.

The sagging Creole cottage was clad in old cypress, the bayou lapping close just behind the property. Hurricanes had chewed the neighborhood more than once; blue tarps still clung to roofs like tired flags, and post-Katrina FEMA trailers lingered nearby.

The air carried a strange perfume of beeswax, pepper smoke, and bloodroot. Inside, the house was tight and uneven, and every doorway its own line of salt and red brick dust. In the front room, vevès drawn in cornmeal spread across the planks—crossroads, suns, spiderwebs.

The mantle was crowned with deer antlers. From the tines dangled gris-gris bundles. An altar nearby bore jars of herbs, bottles of rum, and photographs in chipped frames. Wax dripped thick, cut-glass candle holders.

Frankie paused at the door. "We don't track through the signs," Yvette warned from the back of the house, nodding at a vevè laid across the foyer. "Toe the edges."

Claudia studied the patterns. She didn't believe, but she paid attention. She understood corridors of protection.

Dottie came in last. "If I sneeze and blow one of these out, do the ghosts get in or do I just owe you a new broom?"

Henri and Yvette met them in the front room. Neither asked why they were there. They knew.

Henri caught Claudia's wrist, rolling her sleeve to see the bruise on her arm. Yvette touched the skin with two fingers. A poultice appeared from nowhere—linen damp with camphor and pepper leaves. Yvette pressed it into her hand. "Hold this to the bone. Heat will leave you faster."

Claudia wanted to tell them it was nothing, just a scrape, but their quiet certainty disarmed her. They knew without knowing. "What do I owe you?"

From the hall, an old woman laughed. "You owe respect is what you owe."

She stepped forward. A black skirt tied at her waist, hair wrapped in a headscarf. "I'm Marie-Ange Toussaint. My aunties are here. If you can't behave, that poultice won't neither."

Three women sat in the parlor. On the sideboard: a bottle of Barbancourt, glasses, a plate of saltines dusted with cayenne.

"We brought trouble," Frankie said. "Cash. And receipts." She set an envelope on the sideboard. A shift sheet, a lien search, a gate log. A napkin map. "No names in there. We're not here to buy miracles."

"We don't sell 'em," Marie-Ange said. She didn't touch the envelope. "We make room for the old ones to do their work. If they want to come."

Claudia stood in the doorway, watching the candlelight slick across the chalk lines.

She could feel her mother nearby. She almost said it aloud—come look at this, Mama; look at how carefully they've drawn the world—but the old anger rose and she swallowed it. She didn't come for faith. She came for help you could hold.

Marie-Ange's aunties turned up their cards. A cup. A blade. A road. The woman closest to the mantle hissed softly.

"You got a man in your mouth," she said, pointing at Claudia. "His name tastes like metal."

"Ray," Frankie said.

"Ray," the woman repeated. "A trickster spirit—dangerous and hollow. Shine on him like a new coin, nothing underneath."

Claudia froze. Trickster was truth.

Dottie shifted her weight. "Or, now hear me out, he's a crook with good PR."

"That too," the woman said sweetly. "You say tomato, I say the thing that eats tomatoes from the inside."

Frankie opened the napkin map flat across the table. Each woman leaned in. Names, arrows, roles: Marta Ruiz = courthouse pull; Dottie = filings; Frankie = optics; Claudia = architecture.

The room inhaled, paper bright with dread and order.

Marie-Ange lit another candle. "You bring a picture? I can smell it."

Frankie blinked, then reached into her jacket. She pulled out a glossy from Reese's newsletter—Ray in a blazer, hand on a shovel, Pastor Reese grinning beside him, the ribbon caught mid-flutter. Marie-Ange took it by the corner, held it up to the candle. Wax ran. The ribbon looked like a vein.

"We know a trickster by the shine he wears," Marie-Ange said. "He's got mirror people all around him to make the light jump. Preachers, aldermen, boys who carry envelopes and swear they're doing God's bookkeeping." She lowered the picture to the table. "You want him stopped. Your mama and daddy's old house wants that too. But you don't get to pick the math of none of it."

"What math?" Claudia asked.

"Protection is another ledger," Marie-Ange said simply.

Frankie nodded once. "We'll pay."

"Money is only the easy number," Marie-Ange chuckled, and her aunties made small clucks of agreement. She reached for the envelope then, weighed it in her palm, and set it on the floor, inside a square of cornmeal. She placed the napkin map beside it, careful not to smudge the ink. Names and arrows waited like an unfinished prayer. "You three will stand here," she said, pointing to the edges of the square. "Right foot in. Left foot out. Don't cross the lines with your shadow."

Dottie rolled her eyes, then caught Frankie's sharp look and stepped into place. "Fine," she said. "Right foot, left foot. If a snake shows up to this hokie pokie, I'm kicking the shit out of it."

Marie-Ange smiled. "We prefer diplomacy," she said, and did not look unamused. An auntie reached under the table and tapped Dottie's wrist with something cool and round—a coin, rubbed dark with use—and Dottie snorted.

"No snakes tonight, baby," another auntie chimed in. "Only fishermen and a dog that won't stop howling." She drew a vevè for Legba at the threshold, the cornmeal falling like pale rain.

The aunties began their low hum. Marie-Ange moved through the room as if she were reading blueprints: a wrinkle at the corner of a mouth, a finger pointing to a loose board, the tilt of a candle flame. She lit a new candle and drew it slowly across the cornmeal vevè at her feet, the hot wax hissing where it hit the starch. The geometry held: crossroads, sun, a small trapdoor drawn in flour-white lines.

Frankie's gaze fixed on the shift sheet. Dottie's hand hovered above the lien search, lips pressed thin. Claudia, silent, traced the edge of the gate log, and pressed the gris-gris against her ribs. Each woman claimed her corner, roles locked in place.

Marie-Ange took Frankie's glossy newsletter and held it over the candlelight until the edges blackened. The picture of Ray curled, the ribbon looked obscene. She spoke the name and didn't flinch.

"We know this man to be a trickster spirit now," she said, and the room leaned in as if the words were a forecast. "Shine on him like a new coin. Show his hollowness to any fool who follows his light."

Claudia kept her jaw set. She let Frankie and Dottie nod, let the aunties hum, but she hid her quaking.

Marie-Ange tapped the little bundle she'd given Claudia, then touched Dottie's coin and Frankie's envelope with the tip of her finger. She never said "revenge"—the women avoided that word the way doctors avoid prognosis—but her meaning flexed in the candlelight. "Protection is not a promise the world won't hurt you," she said. "We don't hand you a sword and call it prayer."

Claudia thought of her parents' graves over at Bellande Cemetery—cool stone under liverwort. She thought of pastors' faces in glossy print, of the way a man like Ray could turn a ribbon into a jurisdiction. She didn't want magic to be true. She wanted evidence. Still, when Marie-Ange threaded the thin loop of twine through the gris-gris and slipped it under Claudia's collarbone, she felt the smallest lurch of relief, as if a leak had been plugged somewhere inside her sternum.

"Belief comes later, child." Marie-Ange murmured, reading Claudia's face. "Intention moves the work."

Dottie folded her hands around her coin as if it were already a talisman. Frankie nodded once, the motion like closing a file. The aunties' chant thinned to a single note, and Henri crossed himself at the doorway, a private punctuation. Yvette brushed Claudia's sleeve with a hand that smelled of rosemary and rainwater. "Be careful in the office," she said. "Talk slow. Watch the man with the cheap suit."

They were given instruction: carry the gris-gris where men wouldn't look—inside a bra strap, against a tooth, under a watchband. Leave the envelope inside the cornmeal square for three nights and then press the coin into the grout at the votive on the bar at Frankie's.

Claudia left with the charm inside her bra. The napkin map folded in Frankie's jacket. The case against Ray no longer seemed like chaos; it had a skeletal form now. She didn't feel sanctified—she felt armed.

Outside, the air felt bigger. The night had that cottony hush right before the frogs start. Pepper dust clung to their soles. They crossed and re-crossed their own path—down the walk, a step back, then forward again—like women rehearsing an argument, and when they reached the car, Frankie looked back once and raised a hand. One of the aunties lifted a candle in answer, a small star moving in the window.

Back on the road, Dottie chewed the candied cracker she'd smuggled and clicked the coin in her pocket. Frankie rubbed the heel of her hand against the envelope as if she were feeling the paper's weight translate into plan. Claudia pressed the gris-gris, silent, carrying both the evidence they'd gathered and the fracture she refused to show.

They drove in silence until the road smoothed into the highway. Dottie broke it first.

"I'm not saying I believe, but that house was a helluva lot heavier than it shoulda been."

"Weight is proof," Frankie said.

"Weight is physics," Dottie answered. "Proof is evidence."

Claudia held the gris-gris in her palm. "Evidence is coming," she said. "And if it isn't…"

"…We'll find it," Frankie grinned. Dottie wanted to argue, knowing they had all the proof in the world, and gave her friend a quick squeeze.

They didn't say Ray's name. Names called bad things. The highway unspooled: pines, billboards, black water along the ditch. The candlelight of the Toussaint house stayed with them, a seam of brightness stitched into the rear view.

Fifteen
SHERIFF BUCK

Sheriff Grady "Buck" Harlow stood downtown in the shade of an old live oak, all easy smiles and a slow drawl—your nephew's football coach, your church barbecue's pit boss, the kind of man who called himself simply Buck. He wore his uniform like a good hat: practical, familiar, nonthreatening.

"Quit harassing Brother Ray," Buck told the cluster of neighbors and reporters. "This town ain't for tearing each other up in public. You got a problem, you bring it through the right door."

The crowd scattered. Claudia watched from across the street.

People stared at her. They knew all of Ray's troubles were her fault.

Her late-night calls. The questions in the bar. Frankie's corkboard. Each new slip of paper made Claudia's silence about Ray feel heavier.

Buck's people called it tempering. The rest of the town called it common sense. And the pious called it mercy.

Claudia should have been quieter. She should have let the evidence collect like rain in a gutter. But the house—Bayou House, her parents' pile of peeling siding and probate papers—hummed in her mind like an overdue meter. The will wasn't a neat hourglass; it was a tangle: deeds in both names, a second mortgage unrecorded in the courthouse, a line of credit that matured and then, for reasons she still didn't understand, had been rolled into something called a "development partnership." Every time she moved toward a solution, someone reached across a counter and rerouted the path. Paper trails in Ocean Springs had switchbacks.

Dottie found the first sign. She had a friend in the records department at the hospital, and they went looking for a name in the billing records—small-town clerical cruelty, the kind of thing she was good at—and had come up with a canceled check. The check was from Pastor Reese Ministries; to St. Luke's Medical. Memo line: Harlow—deductible. In this town, generosity had an exchange rate.

Claudia cradled the photocopy like a raw thing. She laid it next to the shift sheet Marta Ruiz had pulled. Together they looked less like stray papers and more like a ledger starting to balance. She thought of Buck bending over the barbecue, his boy at his side, the fundraisers that always had the right soup and the right smile. She thought of the quiet gratitude that turned hooked men into indebted men. The sheriff's benefactor was a church leader. That created obligation.

Claudia pushed the photocopy across the clerk's counter. The woman behind the plexiglass looked at the paper, then at Claudia, then away.

"You don't need to ask about Sheriff Buck, honey," the woman said finally. Her badge read Elena. She folded her hands. "People already think you're stirring up too much shit."

"I need to know who signed it," Claudia said. "Why would Pastor Reese be paying someone's deductible?"

The woman pursed her lips and leaned forward. "Buck's boy, Grady Jr.—they covered his chemo last year. Whole town knew about it. They didn't want the pity party, so Pastor Reese sent money to the hospital and told us to code it as assistance. Said it'd be easier on everyone. No press, no paperwork for the paper. Give the family a break, that's what he said."

"They brought casseroles," Elena went on. "The church van came twice a week. Ladies from the ministry signed up for rides. Someone slipped envelopes into the intake nurse's pocket after the funeral they didn't hold. You don't see duffel bags on pews—you see casserole pans and house calls and people who owe the ones who gave them soup."

"So it's just bribing a sheriff off with charity?" Claudia said.

Elena snorted. "We all got debts. Somebody got to keep this town afloat."

"Pastor Reese pays a deductible, Buck turns down the heat on an illegal shelter. Nice and clean. But clean don't mean honest."

The napkin map now had Sheriff Buck's name inked in. A sheriff bound not by cash but by soup spoons and chemo rides.

A lawman who could look away without being asked.

"So they keep it quiet," Claudia said.

"They always do," Elena said. "Churches are good at that sort of thing. You don't hear about it until someone like you starts asking the wrong people the right questions."

Claudia left the hospital with the photocopy and a new understanding: this was not a cartoon ledger with a villain and a duffel. It was quieter and worse—an economy of kindness that bought silence and rewired obligation. She found herself wondering, for the first time in days, whether she'd been cruel or reckless. She had come for a clear line.

What she found was rope.

And somewhere in that weave, someone had already used it for a noose.

Claudia felt the braid tighten around her throat.

"Law's not just bought," she told Frankie that night in the back office, voice low enough that the street heard nothing. "It's owed. And debts in a town like this come with conditions you can't litigate away."

Frankie's cigarette smoke made a halo. "So we choke or we choke the rope," she said. Her words were blunt because blunt was a tool. Dottie sat at the table, elbows up, the coin in her pocket making a private noise. The shift sheet, the lien search, the gate log—all spread on the desk like a battlefield map. Each woman claimed her piece.

Claudia's silence about Ray stayed folded, hidden.

The next morning, they headed over to probate court.

"Probate's backed up," the clerk said, fat index finger marking a schedule. "Nine to twelve months before deeds are clearing. And if anyone contests—well."

"Too bad, right?" Claudia said. "Thanks so much."

She would allow herself a year. A year to get Bayou House in order. A year suspended between grief and bureaucracy.

Claudia walked out of the courthouse and spotted a bench. The sun felt like something that didn't belong to her. She leaned back and thought, with unusual clarity: Fuck all of this.

She had wanted the estate settled so she could cut ties clean—sell the house, pay the hospice bills, lock a door and breathe. Instead she was standing under Buck's soft sermon and Pastor Reese's quiet generosity and a check that read like a sentence.

She questioned herself. Is this obsession, or is it evidence? Is this courage, or is it compulsion?

She knew it was both.

That night she opened the kitchen drawer. Her mother's recipes were there. A postcard. In the margin, her mother had written: Be careful who you call family.

Claudia set the photocopy of the hospital check on the counter and breathed until the room stopped rocking. Then she laid Marta Ruiz's filings beside it, the napkin map folded on top. A case file taking shape—no longer chaos, but architecture drawn in pencil and dread.

She was not a crusader.

She fell asleep at the kitchen table with her head on her arms.

When she woke she felt the edge of something new—not a plan, not yet, but a scale tipping. The town liked its stories simple. So did she, sometimes. But complexity had the shape of her parents' bills, a rotting house, and complexity would not be outmaneuvered by good intentions and polite crowds.

She stood, wiped her face with the heel of her hand, and started imagining another string on Frankie's corkboard. Napkin map expanded, roles set, the women tightening chaos into a net. In its empty center hung the thing none of them said aloud: someone would pay for all this before it was over.

Sixteen

ECHOES

Bayou House always smelled of slow cookers and smoke. The altar in the corner, once cluttered with candles and recipe cards and the little things Claudia's mother left like small demands, had been wiped clean.

The new order felt deliberate—lines imposed on chaos, tools laid out before a job.

Claudia hadn't seen Ray since Pastor Reese and Margaret Ann had paid his bail. They owned him now, and she hated that she missed him. She didn't expect to find him on her porch at two in the morning, hunched against the rail in a hoodie taking a drag on a glass bowl of weed.

"Ray?"

He looked up. His face was scrubbed raw; the beard had gone from negligent to deliberate.

"You look like you've been living in a swamp," she said before she could catch herself.

He laughed once, tapping the bowl on the railing. "I am."

"Tent's up past the cattails. Swamp's got better plumbing than a lotta houses."

"Why are you back? Reese got you out. Margaret Ann got you out. Don't you dare play the victim."

"Yeah." He took a long drag. "I coulda stayed at Margaret Ann's for a night, or on Reese's couch. But I don't like borrowed rooms." He looked past her through the doorway at the erased altar. "I just didn't wanna bring mud back over here."

"You could have called. I wanted to know you were okay."

He looked at her then with something like practiced bravado. "I know." He pinched the bridge of his nose. "I thought if I disappeared you'd stop getting tagged to me. Maybe folks'd stop lookin' at you… maybe you'd stop catching heat."

"You fucking vanished," she said. "Not even a simple I'm sorry. People started blaming me… Said I was the one trying to get you pinched."

"Aren't you?"

She held up her broken arm. "Fuck you, Ray."

He snorted. "People'll say what people want. Sheriff's got his own problems. They all do. That's why I went to the swamp."

"You're going to live in a tent?"

"Until it don't anymore," he said. "Until something's left to go back to."

"Or until I make something I can live in."

Claudia stepped closer, the porch boards protesting under her weight. He smelled of smoke and swamp and the faint marine tang of a life lived outside windows. Up close she could see the rawness of him—a bruise near his jaw, a cut near the knuckle.

"You look like shit," she said.

"You look like guilt," he said, a half-grin that didn't reach his eyes. "You're the one who's been carrying it. I tried to lighten your load."

"You ran. Coward." He flinched.

"Yeah. I ran." He met her then, steady as a plank.

His hoodie shifted, showing the healed outline of a needle-track on his arm.

Claudia hated that her eyes went straight to the details anyway. "You could have called me a coward and I still would've come."

"You talk like you want me to be less dangerous," he said, voice quiet. "But you like the shine I wear. You know that."

"I don't like what you are," she said. "I like what you try to be. Half of it's all noise.

Half of it's… I don't know."

He dropped his eyes. "You don't have to know. I don't want you to change for me."

"But I miss you. And I—" He paused.

"You're not supposed to make me say it," she said.

"Say what?"

"You're a mess," she said. "You make me angry and I think you're an idiot and sometimes I want to hit you. And I still love you, fucker."

He stopped breathing for a minute, just staring at her.

Then his face cracked into an unholy grin. "That's the nicest thing I've ever been called," he said.

He reached for her. She let him.

"And just for the record," he began. "I didn't kill the McKinnons."

"I know. Doesn't make you a good person. Was it Ice?"

He didn't answer.

They sat on the porch rail, shoulder to shoulder, the bowl between them and smoke drifting up into the dark. He told her about the tent—the tarp, the way the swamp sang at night, the company of frogs.

She told him about probate and receipts and the way the town was folding in on itself with all the evangelical corruption. She told him they were using him. That he was a pawn.

She didn't tell him about the role she'd taken on the team—architect of the paper skeleton—or the fault line with his name under it.

When he stood to leave, he hesitated. "I'm not asking you to forgive me," he said. "I just want you to know I came back."

"You came back," she said. It was not absolution.

It was all the fragile currency they had to work with.

He tucked the bowl back into his pocket and slipped into the night.

Claudia watched him go—a shape against the cattails as she let the door shut with a soft, decisive click.

• • •

At the bar the next morning, Frankie held a stack of receipts strapped with a nicotine-stained rubber band. She spread them across the backroom counter. The napkin network map covered everything—names and arrows, each woman's role inked at the margin: FRANKIE = optics & ops; DOTTIE = filings & pulls; CLAUDIA = architecture & timelines.

"Look at this," she said. "May 14th. $9,980. Deposit location—Magnolia Crown Casino. Cage Drawer #7—TL."

She lined the slip up with a chip voucher from the same day, timestamped 11:42 p.m., voucher number 004771. Same hand on the back of the voucher: "cash out—float."

Claudia bent over the counter, eyes fast on the columns. She liked numbers because they didn't lie in the soft ways people did; they bent toward ledger logic, and you could make them talk if you laid enough of them end to end.

"They're doing the float," she said. "They park chips for a night, then cash them out in small increments so the CTRs don't trip." She said it like a mechanic explaining oil pressure, not a zealot indicting sin. "Same amounts, same casinos, same cadence. $9,980. Someone's teaching them to hug just under the wire."

What bothered her was the same number showing up just below it, over and over again. That was called structuring, and she knew it was a federal crime.

Casinos weren't blind to this either: the cage was supposed to flag odd patterns, file suspicious activity reports, and keep records of large chip buys and cash-outs. Claudia knew the net wasn't only a $10,000 line—it was paperwork thick as kudzu, and the pattern wriggled through it.

Frankie pulled another paper free, this one an escrow addendum for the McKinnon property. The line item read: BBM Consult Fee—$27,500—Paid via wire to: Crown Holdings, LLC—Ref: McKinnon Addendum 5/15. The wire confirmation number was stamped in micro-print, the routing bleeding into smudged ink. The seller had listed a $15,000 "consult," suddenly jumped to $27,500 in the addendum. The same day: a $9,980 cash-in at Magnolia Crown; a cluster of benevolence checks from Pastor Reese's ledger that balanced against BBM account transfers.

"I want that clerk's name," Claudia said. "Who signed this? Who notarized it?" Her voice had the flatness of someone moving a pry bar; she meant to get leverage, not sermons.

Frankie had a list. She read it off without looking up, one name at a time like a prayer at the wrong kind of funeral. "Marta Ruiz—Title Clerk, Coastal Title & Trust. Cage cashier—Trey Langston, Magnolia

Crown, Cage Drawer #7. Gate security—night shift: Hollis P. on the subdivision log, copied by Marta. BBM account manager—one Ray Broussard., alias on file: BBM Partners. Wire sent to Crown Holdings, registered at a PO box in Gautier."

Claudia wrote the names on her palm and then on a sticky note, the letters quick: MARTA RUIZ. TREY LANGSTON. HOLLIS P. (GATE LOG). CROWN HOLDINGS. Each name felt like a nail.

"You plant those names," Frankie said, meaning it. "You get a subpoena, you get them on the stand, you get their signatures to mean something other than ink." She flicked the voucher with a quick, impatient thumb. "We seed testimony. You can't un-ring a bell."

Dottie wandered in with a half-smile and a thermos of coffee. "You planting seeds or digging graves?" She asked, because she liked metaphors less prissy than Frankie did.

"You a grave digger or a gardener?" Frankie countered. "Pick."

"Both," Dottie said, and dropped a folder. Inside: photocopies of benevolence fund checks, Pastor Reese's initials on deposit tapes, a ledger from St. Luke's with entries coded as "charity" that matched a string of deposits into BBM accounts. She slid over a fresh lien search, Marta's pull stamped at the bottom.

Claudia felt the room shift. They had receipts, not indictments—yet. Receipts were paper scaffolding, proof that something had been put into motion. Her finger went to the margins where one of the benevolence checks had a faint stamp: RECEIVED: Magnolia Crown Casino — Cage Drawer #7 — TL. Trey Langston's initials again. It was the same choreography repeated: tithes into plates, plates into BBM, BBM into chip float, chip float into Crown, Crown into cash, cash into "consults" that showed up on a deed.

They built cases out of repetition, not Hollywood bank robberies. That's what made it meaner: it was lawful-adjacent, legal veneer on a plumbing job.

Frankie called them "echoes." The phrase stuck because it sounded both inevitable and ridiculous. "They don't do threats in the movies anymore," she said. "Now they follow you. They make your car feel watched. They make the clerk nervous. They show up at your kid's soccer game with casserole and a smile. They use kindness like a leash."

Claudia had read cases once about intimidation that didn't scream: the man who stood at an ex-wife's PTA meeting and asked about alimony, the contractor who dropped a quote that included a favor for 'a friend of the family,' the anonymous letter that arrived with a key to a safe deposit box. It was all stairs instead of sledgehammers. It took patience. It was suffocating.

On the way out of the bar, Claudia glanced at the street. A black Suburban with out-of-state plates eased past and slowed. The driver's face was a shadow.

It made her stomach drop. She moved, tried the door handle of the car, turned the key, and drove.

She felt followed.

Later, she would learn the model of that Suburban matched two other tails—one that had driven past the Toussaint house the week before, one that had paused opposite Frankie's bar the night an envelope had disappeared from behind the register.

"We're picking up too much attention," Dottie said in a voice made small by the parking lot lights. She clicked the coin in her pocket as if it were an offering to luck. "If they want us watching, then we watch right back. Cameras, route logs, time stamps—not prayer beads."

Marie-Ange's aunties had practical advice too.

"If someone pays attention to your footsteps, make your footsteps mean something else."

They taught Claudia how to switch routes, ride with other drivers, use public spaces for meetings. They could burn incense into shrewd tactics. Protection, they said, had nothing to do with mysticism alone—sometimes it was a second phone and a friend who could pick up a tail.

Back in the back office, they set a trap that was more trellis than net. Frankie called in a favor from a waitress who worked the Magnolia Crown's poker room. The waitress agreed to e-mail a scanned shift sheet showing who had been working cage drawer #7 on the nights of the deposits. It was shaky—employees got fired for less in casino towns—but it was a shot. Claudia would not seize it yet; she would braid it into something longer. She pinned the shift sheet to the corkboard.

They found a cell phone receipt that spoke in dots and lies: a prepaid flip phone bought in Pascagoula three days before a deposit spike, activation at 9:14 p.m., calls to a number associated with BBM partners until 1:03 a.m., then silence. That was the kind of breadcrumb that could be traced, but it required subpoenas and patience—two things the town did not hand out quickly.

And there were the softer intimations. A voicemail on Claudia's burner: heavy breathing, then a man clearing his throat. No words. The message hung in her phone like a punctuation mark. "Quit harassing Brother Ray," Buck's voice might say to a crowd. On a voicemail, you got the flavor of it—an edge. Someone wanted them to know they were noticed.

Claudia slept in fits that week, her arm throbbing, the gris-gris warm against her sternum and the Suburban's shadow in the crook of her dreams. She woke with receipts in her hand and a plan in her head, a way to move names from paper to public. Marta Ruiz and Trey Langston became more than letters: they were people who could be subpoenaed, frightened, convinced, or bought. Frankie would handle the calls. Dottie would pull the filings. Claudia would stage the timeline. Each woman took her post;

Claudia kept Ray's fault line hidden under the neatness.

They were closer. The receipts were an echo of a mechanism now audible: the float, the consults, the benevolence ledgers. They were starting to see where the pipes fed the surface. But the pipes were not wood and copper; they were men's favors and church vans and quiet hospital donations folded into something that looked like virtue.

If the Dixie Mafia's rhythm was a heartbeat, this was the place where you could hear it: patient, slow, and entirely ordinary. You could poke it and see no blood, only a careful pattern of kindnesses wired into consequence. It was meaner because it passed as mercy.

They would need evidence that could stand in court: signed sheets, ledger stamps, witnesses who could swear under oath. For now, they had noise and a neighborhood that watched them like a ledger watches numbers. For now, that was enough to make them move smarter.

The Suburban passed their bar again two nights after the voicemail. This time, Frankie's headlights found it first. Instead of driving away, she watched the windows like a hawk until the vehicle turned and left. She called Claudia, who answered on the second ring, voice a notch lower than usual.

"We're being read," Frankie said. "They're testing us."

Claudia looked at the pile of receipts. She thought of Bayou House and of a pile of probate papers that had been a rope around her for months. She thought of her parents' ghosts and of the menu of favors that had kept a child alive and a sheriff gentle.

"Let them test it," Claudia said. "We don't let them make the rules."

Outside, the bar's neon hummed. The receipts lay like bones on the counter, and somewhere across the water the Magnolia Crown glittered like a quiet promise. The map on the wall kept growing—names, roles, arrows—order stitched over fear. In the margins, an absence waited for a name, the kind of blank that ends with a body.

Claudia silently hoped it wouldn't be Ray taking the fall for the rich and powerful.

Seventeen
BLOOD PRICE

Frankie shut the backroom door and the room narrowed into a map of four faces and a single bulb. Dottie had binders. Lila had a sling bag. Claudia had the photocopies from the hospital with the sticky notes creeping from the edges, and, folded into her palm like a secret, the gris-gris Marie-Ange had tied. Beneath it all lay the napkin network map, taped to the counter—names, arrows, and timeslots marching in order where fear wanted noise.

"Alright," Frankie said. "We're not going to play hero. We're going to play surgeon. Cut the artery, stop the bleed."

"Roles?"

Dottie answered. "Records. Bonds. Court pulls. If something's filed, I'll find it."

She pushed a binder forward. "I'll start tomorrow at municipal, then the county, then the hospital admin. If we need subpoenas, I'll figure the angles." She clipped in Marta Ruiz's latest pulls—lien search, title addendum copies—and a photocopy of the subdivision gate log, Hollis P.'s initials circled.

Frankie made a small satisfied sound. "You're the spine, Dots. Keep us honest."

"Infiltration," Lila said. "I'll get friendly with Trey—Trey Langston—see who's on cashouts, who flirts with who. I can work the cage, hang with cocktail waitresses, get a shift sheet. I'm not above spilling coffee on someone's lap if it gets me a name." She grinned.

"I can meet the ministry volunteers under the pretense of Sunday school sign-ups. Someone's got to be the shadow that sees what the ledger does between lines." She slid a phone onto the map: a clean burner set to photograph and forward shift sheets the moment they print.

Claudia listened and felt a steadiness in their voices that steadied the jitter in her chest. "Frankie does the money map," she said. "Connections, floats, chip vouchers, timing. Lila gets access points on the ground. Dottie gives us the documentary backbone." She spoke in shorthand because the list needed to be executable. "We seed testimony—Marta Ruiz, Trey Langston. Get a waitress e-mail, a shift sheet, a wire confirmation. We push the ledger into the light." She penciled her own box on the map:

CLAUDIA—architecture & timeline; kept the line that should have read RAY blank.

Frankie pushed the escrow across to Claudia and let the light catch the memo line. "Reese and Margaret Ann bail him out because mercy is a better headline than silence. It buys them optics, utility, and leverage. He owes them. He's a useful idiot."

Frankie's voice went colder. "And when the ledger needs a blood price, who's expendable? The guy whose face reads worst in print."

Names sketched across a napkin: Whitcomb, Reilly, Reese, Margaret Ann, Trey Langston, Marta Ruiz, Crown Holdings, BBM Partners. Frankie circled Ray in the middle.

"Why would they hang him out?" Lila asked, and the room smelled of coffee and the braid of a question turning into a plan.

"Because Ray's expendable," Frankie said. "Because Ray makes them money and eats their guilt and he's the kind of man whose face is useful in a press photo when you need to show restitution. They know they can sacrifice Ray to keep their machine clean. That's how Dixie works the God machine."

Dottie tapped the binder with a fingernail. "And because the town doesn't see the money pipeline. They see salvation. They'll forgive a pastor who signs a check but they'll burn a man with a rap sheet."

"We aim low," she continued. "We break Ray from the pipeline. Get him out of town. Let 'em all choke."

She slid forward a quiet request form: title-search expansions, lien continuations, gate-log subpoenas drafted in pencil.

Frankie tapped the folder until the paper stung, then pushed the escrow addendum across the counter like a card you didn't want to look at twice. "Think about what Ray actually is to them," she said. "He trades in people, faces, favors. He brings boots when they need muscle, stories when they need cover, a photo op when they need a human front. He moves cash because he knows whom to trust and whom to burn."

Claudia felt a coldness settle under her ribs at the thought of ejecting Ray, of using him as a lever to dismantle machinery she could not otherwise pry loose. The gris-gris in her palm was a small, ridiculous warmth against that cold—too slight to be religion, too honest to be nothing. She thought of his porch and the swamp tarp, the way he'd said he'd run so she wouldn't get trailed; she thought, differently, of the glossy photos and the receipts that smelled like rust. She hated that she reduced him to leverage and hated more the way Reese could give and still reserve the right to take. She pressed the twine at her collarbone and said nothing about the apartment over the garage. Order required silence; silence carried risk.

She glanced at the women around the table—Frankie's blunt hands, Dottie's binder-thick patience, Lila's calm, dangerous grace—and felt something like faith, small and sharp. Gods had never signed checks for her parents; the platitudes she'd been raised on —God provides— had felt thin the day hospice bills came. Now her rites were practical: binders, subpoenas, late-night stakeouts. The gris-gris felt less like a prayer than a pact stitched in thread: you will not do this alone.

"We break the visible nodes," she said, and the words were less a command than a confession. "We drive the optics—make them look like they're saving the town by getting rid of one of their own. Meanwhile we go after the wiring: title clerks, consult fees, Crown Holdings. We will not let a single name be left unasked." She slid the photocopy back across the counter; under the bulb the ink looked like a map. The women nodded, and for the first time in a long while Claudia felt that thin, dangerous faith—faith in them. Fear met its counterweight: women assigning themselves to corners, counting the screws.

They planned like that into the night—small operations nested inside small operations. Lila would volunteer at the ministry's soup runs; Dottie would pull anyone who'd signed receipts for "benevolence" drives; Frankie would map timing anomalies and set up a meeting with a poker-room waitress who'd text receipt photos when she could. They arranged benches, safe houses, a burner line Claudia kept in the gris-gris's small pocket tucked against her sternum. On the map's margin, Frankie inked a schedule: SHIFT SHEET (Cage #7) ☒ GATE LOG CROSS-CHECK ☒ LIEN CONTINUATIONS.

By the end of the night, Claudia made a decision she didn't tell the others. Not into the house. Not in her bed. But in the apartment over the garage. A mattress, blankets, a chair.

It kept him off the swamp floor and gave him a place to wash without stealing space inside the rooms that still smelled like her mother. Ray promised to keep his people thin—two, maybe three at most. He kept that promise. The entourage that had surrounded him before—boys with open hands and easier loyalties—didn't return. For a week, they saw him once in the market, once on the porch, twice deep in the diner where sour coffee lingered. It gave Claudia hope in the brittle way hope comes when you let yourself close your eyes and forget reality for a second. She filed the choice under logistics, not confession.

She didn't tell them. It was a sin of omission she was comfortable with.

She told herself it was tactical—liabilities multiply when you add people—and another, smaller truth: having him close made her feel less feral. She admitted, in the private ledger of her thoughts, that his nearness dulled the raw edge of grief—a small, shameful comfort, not strategy.

Some of the homeless started to grumble. They'd been Ray's armor.

Lately, they said cutthroat things in low voices: maybe the shine was bait; maybe Ray was using them. A woman named Bess spat, "He playin' us, honey. He got us to hold the rope while they climb."

The hospice of suspicion was dangerous; it suggested a loss of loyalty that would make policing easier on the other side. They needed proof the soft armor was thinning—and proof arrived in the small, mean gestures that mattered more than chest-thumping.

At the feed-truck a man named Marlow folded his tent. He didn't say goodbye.

A younger man, called Snake for his quick hands, stepped past the line when Frankie held out a paper plate; he shook his head and walked on, eyes fixed on the road as if looking for a way out. No shouting, no scenes—just the quiet business of people who'd stopped believing the promise that had kept them warm.

When people began folding tents or turning down a plate, it wasn't simple betrayal; it was a reconfiguration of the net that had kept some of them alive. For Claudia, that shift was the clearest proof yet that the pipeline ran not just through banks but through people's lives. The map on Frankie's wall added a new ring: SOFT ARMOR EROSION ⊠ optics leverage.

Later, when Ray drifted through the lot, a man who'd once taken his hand looked him in the eye and said, "Not today," then turned away.

Claudia heard that and felt the knot tighten. Small betrayals were the machine's favorite weather: they looked like choice, not coercion. If the homeless started folding tents and skipping meals, then Ray's visible cover would shrink softly, as if someone were erasing his outline in pencil. That erasure would make it easier for a crowd—and for the law—to say the pipeline had been only one man's doing. That was leverage the machine understood.

They updated the aim over another scotch and a folded napkin: Break Ray from the pipeline. Get him out of town. Expose the consults. Compel testimony. Win optics. The list read like a war plan and tasted like obsession. Frankie underlined TIMELINE and pinned a fresh shift-sheet ask; Dottie queued lien continuations; Lila scheduled the poker-room handoff; Claudia re-inked the arrows and kept Ray's line invisible.

They assigned small tasks with surgical care. Lila would have the soup-run register keyed for her contact who waited tables at Magnolia Crown. Dottie would file a quiet lien search on Crown Holdings and pull Marta Ruiz's title-clerk history. Frankie would set a meet with a woman who once cashed out suspiciously large vouchers and had a habit of gossiping when she'd had too many hours of overtime. Claudia would keep Ray near and invisible, a watcher and a ward. Women imposing order: one rhythm, four corners.

They left the bar in a line, mouths set, pockets filled with paper and a smell of conspiracy. On the porch, they paused, each woman finding the curve of the night before going back into the world. Frankie's hand brushed Claudia's shoulder—no words, only pressure.

She watched him duck inside, the apartment door closing soft behind him, and for a long moment she stood on the driveway with the blanket folded in her hands. She had let him back into a roof and a cot and that was practical mercy; it was also survival.

He had never apologized for breaking her arm.

She remembered the way the bone had bitten through the skin, the hospital's white light, the slow, humiliating work of learning to trust her left hand again. She had never asked for an apology; she'd wanted safety, accounting, a reckoning that meant he would not do it twice. His absence had been penance of a sort; his quiet return felt like a truce without terms. And she hated that she still loved him.

She wrote "APOLOGY (ABSENT)" on a receipt.

Claudia folded the thin blanket into a neat square, tucked it under her arm, and walked back to her car with that unclosed line between them warming like a bruise.

When she walked toward the house, a lone security light cast the apartment window into a square of gold. She told herself she'd tell the women in the morning—that she'd been honest before a plan moved to its sharper edge. She did not. The omission was a small thing then, a private arithmetic. It would become a fault line.

Eighteen
PRAY TO PLAY

Lila no longer smelled like her usual patchouli and incense: she smelled like Windex. She had come early to arrange hymnals and help clean. She'd practiced the opening line—"I heard about your ministry—my sister needs a meal."

Now seated in a middle pew, her eyes drifted to Trey Langston. Trey was the man who signed the chip vouchers, who initialed the cage drawer tapes, the one whose initials sometimes appeared faintly on deposit slips labeled "benevolence."

If Trey decided you were trouble, a dealer's time card could go missing, a voucher could be "misfiled," and a wire reconciliation would never point to the names. Row after row of locals she knew didn't have a place to call home. They sat together.

The pastor led the liturgy. He asked the congregation: Do you repent? Do you commit? Will you stand with your neighbor in time of need? Lila hated this part. She knew the rules: no penitence, no bed. Miss a service, miss a meal.

Classic pray to play, she thought. She hated conditional charity.

When he asked for new members to rise and swear the loyalty oath—a casual thing, legal in five states, spiritual in twenty—Lila's hand twitched. She felt the burner phone at her hip and kept her face still. She didn't rise. She wouldn't give them that much.

The pastor's eyes found her. Trey smiled the sort of tight smile lawyers wear, and an old woman two pews down caught Lila's face and nodded, half-congratulating, half-questioning. Everyone had a cadence for newcomers and traitors; the line between the two was sometimes thinner than a hymn line.

In the back, Claudia worried about her friend. She had told Lila to breathe, to answer only what was asked. No more. Claudia watched the pastor press for names, for a public "I will." Lila's jaw locked as he stared at her expectantly.

"Come on now, sister, rise and say it," Lila's fingers went slack in her lap. A bead of sweat caught at her temple.

She was an easy mark. One wrong second and Trey would remember her, too.

Claudia noticed, and moved. She made her way up the aisle in long steps and leaned over Lila, the motion casual, the tilt practiced.

"What did you say in the foyer?" she whispered loud enough for the pews to hear, as if rehearsing a sermon line. "About the soup ministry? I'd like to help sign people up."

The pastor blinked. Heads turned, including Trey Langston. The old ladies tutted: busybody at work. Trey's smile thinned. Lila's color returned like someone had turned on a faucet. She stood, murmured a sisterly "I will," and the pastor's hand came down.

Claudia breathed once. "Get the receipts," she whispered. "We don't give them a headline—only paper."

Later, in the parking lot, Claudia approached Lila. "That was close," Claudia said. "You shoulda just stood up. It's all an act, anyway."

Lila didn't disagree. "I was listening, not performing. I had to make not look deliberate."

"You stood out." Claudia said. "Sometimes just be part of the flock."

Lila's jaw tightened. She hated organized religion. "I did what I had to." She exhaled, role intact: Infiltration holds.

Claudia's phone vibrated: a text—three words, none of them soft. Here. Alley. Now.

"Give us five," she texted back.

The men in the Suburbans had been a presence in town for weeks. They tail, they take notes, they wear plain faces that fit any civic parade. Everyone understood what it cost to be watched by a car with no name. Frankie texted back a plate number; Claudia wrote it next to "Gate Log—Hollis P." to cross-check later.

Dottie led them behind the bait shop. The alley was half-light and wet cardboard.

The man from the Suburban offered her a cigarette.

Dottie took it, struck a match, and tapped the flame out against her hand. "Who sent you?"

"Just curious," he said. "Seems there's a lot of unhappy folks poking around."

"Curiosity's expensive," Dottie said.

His laugh changed. He gave her a place—"Gulfport"—and then a name.

Dottie stepped in close, blocking Claudia's view with her shoulder. Claudia saw the man's posture go wrong. She heard voices. Then a sound she didn't want to catalog.

Fifteen minutes later the man walked out fast, collar crooked, eyes fixed on anywhere but Dottie.

Dottie watched him go. "You tell your boss he'll get one more nice day," she said. "After that, folks are gonna be a lot less charitable."

Dottie wanted it to look like a warning; the story would reach Gulfport first. "Fuck around and find out."

On the ride back, nobody talked.

Claudia kept her eyes on the dashboard clock. She wanted to write down what Dottie had just done, because writing made things orderly. She didn't. Some facts didn't belong on paper yet.

At a stoplight, Lila flexed her fingers once, like she was bleeding off adrenaline.

"That name," Lila said.

"Yeah," Claudia said.

She didn't add anything else. She didn't need to. Dottie had just moved the line, and they all felt where it was now.

By the time they got back to the bar, Claudia's head was running contingencies.

If Trey sniffed Lila out, the shift sheets evaporated.

If anyone had a photo of Dottie in that alley, they didn't have a problem—they had a case.

If Ray's garage apartment leaked, it didn't just bruise optics. It broke the plan and worse, their trust in Claudia.

And the Suburban boys—Gulfport—meant this wasn't only town business anymore. Outside eyes. Patient ones.

She left one square blank where Ray belonged and felt it staring back at her. She told herself it was temporary. That the lie was easy.

She wrote small margin notes—contingencies embedded in sentences: Lila lies low; Dottie files a false lead; Ray stays invisible until the optics shift; feed runs move to other hands.

The napkin fit into the gris-gris's pocket like a secret folded into a charm. The inventory didn't make her feel clever; it made her feel steadier, as if naming the fires might keep them from leaping. It was also an admission: they were playing with fire. Exposure demanded better choreography.

When Dottie came back, she smelled of cigarette smoke and cheap cologne and the faint, stubborn tang of victory. Her hands were dark at the knuckles from scrubbing something off; she didn't look apologetic. She sat, uncapped the thermos, and took a long, deliberate swallow.

"You okay?" Lila asked.

Dottie's grin was a proud slash. "Yeah," she said. "He'll think twice before he takes pictures he ain't supposed to. Useful day. Sent a message back to Gulfport." Frankie logged the time and plate on the wall, a quiet drumbeat toward subpoenas.

Claudia watched her, watched the thermos steam like a small altar. She knew the ledger: favors bought and favors owed; sons on chemo and small kindnesses that acted like chains. She'd given Ray a shelf over the garage for mercy and found that mercy had a price. And now she'd learned Dottie carried her own scale. Women, four corners; roles fixed; the caper arc climbing.

"We pivot," Frankie said. "Enough mapping—time to burn it down."

Claudia looked at the blank square again. She folded the napkin and slid it into the gris-gris pocket.

"October twelfth," Frankie said.

Nineteen
RITUAL OF SHADOWS

The night vibrated with cicadas and nearby generators. Smoke moved through the trees. Tonight, the house listened. The Toussaints moved barefoot across the warped boards and down into Claudia's yard.

Henri carried a Djembe drum and a nylon bag filled with totems and offerings in mason jars. Yvette followed with paper sacks of roots and bones tied up with ribbons. Bending low in the dirt at the foot of the house, Henri scratched a vevè into the soil with an oyster shell.

The rhythm started slow. Then faster. Henri beat the drum like hooves across shallow water. Candles spat. Smoke wound into the scent of rum and sage. The house creaked in time with the rhythm.

Claudia stood at the edge, and the visions came: ancient Creole, Spanish, and French with rotten teeth; modern meth-thin men she recognized from local shelters; hard-living women with sores that never healed—no distance between them, all waiting for the same thing.

Ray wasn't supposed to be here. But he'd emerged from the garage saying his ministry needed to "partner" with the old ways.

"There he goes again," Dottie rolled her eyes.

Claudia caught his eye across the circle. "You want forgiveness," she said.

Ray leaned forward, sweat shining on his lip. "We all need it."

"Not like you do," Frankie said, pointing a long finger.

None of them understood the bloodwater between her and Ray. Claudia didn't care if they didn't.

The drums rose until Ice stepped inside the vevè. The rhythm faltered, Henri hit off-beat. The smoke reversed direction. Shutters clapped. The ritual recoiled.

Claudia felt the circle contract. Whatever the ritual had been moving toward was now paused, held in place by the simple fact of a body where it shouldn't be.

Dottie's eyes snapped to him first. Her hand twitched toward her buck knife.

Ray lifted his hands. "He belongs," he said. "Ice needs this as much as we do. Maybe more."

Claudia understood then that Ray hadn't brought Ice for protection or belief. He had brought him to be seen bringing him. Dragging a parolee into drumlight was proof of gospel. If Ice walked away changed, maybe the town would believe Ray was, too. Maybe he could outrun the ghosts of men he'd buried.

But the circle wasn't convinced. Claudia's visions wavered.

Henri stopped the drum and let the silence sit. He looked at Ice, then at Ray, then back to Ice again. "You crossed without invitation," he said. "That puts you under this house, not inside it."

Ray opened his mouth, but Henri raised one finger and didn't look at him. "Nothing happens tonight," he said. "But boy, you sure started something."

Ray nodded once. Ice glared at Ray, realizing he was being used, not redeemed. The circle did not break. It loosened. That was worse.

Dottie's jaw locked. If the ghosts wanted blood tonight, Ice had just volunteered it.

Frankie watched the breach and ran the numbers on a likely body count.

Claudia watched Ice intently. He carried himself like someone who knew where the exits were. Fresh out of Angola Prison, his posture gave him away—still measuring rooms, still waiting for a door to close. His face settled as Henri'a drum stopped. Whatever he'd come for, it hadn't been forgiveness.

Lila lingered at the edge of the circle. She didn't move closer, but she didn't step back either.

Then Caroline stepped into the circle—barefoot, her hand brushing her sister's. Her touch steadied her.

The drums climbed higher. The Toussaints chanted. No prophecy came—only crossroads.

Beyond the circle, the houses stayed dark. No one came closer. No one left.

Henri gathered the cloth and wrapped the drum. Yvette snuffed the candles one by one. No blessing. No dismissal. People drifted off without speaking, careful not to look at Ice or Ray too long.

They each knew that by morning, Ice would not be welcome back at Bayou House. Not barred. Just understood. He would be watched if he returned.

Ray would babble about the ritual as a new covenant. The Toussaints would not correct him. They would also not answer his calls or texts.

Claudia knew better now. What happened there next would not be spiritual. It would be practical.

Frankie would mark Ice as unstable and Ray as compromised. Dottie would add both names to a list she hadn't shown anyone yet.

Nothing had been forgiven. Nothing had been decided.

When the last drumbeat cracked, silence fell. Fireworks burst over Biloxi. The smell of sulfur drifted downwind and mixed with sage smoke across the water.

Bayou House shuddered.

Twenty

SIEGE

Dottie showed up at Bayou House before sunrise with a Rubbermaid tote full of cameras and began climbing up a ladder with a drill. Henri appeared too, wanting to help.

"We don't need eyes, Dottie. We need peace." Caroline stood by the doorway, prayer beads around her wrist before walking back inside. Claudia was at the kitchen sink, coffee cold in her hands.

Dottie nodded at Henri. "He thinks last night didn't count."

Henri smiled once. Not kindly.

"You don't tug a gate and pretend it stays shut," he said.

Dottie snorted. "Ray don't believe in gates."

"Everybody believes," Henri said. "Some people just learn late who they been talking to."

Ray's voice interrupted, threading through the Spanish moss like someone trying to thread a needle with a rope.

"You all been sleeping on me," he rasped toward a couple of homeless residents who remained in the yard.

"You been hidin' behind forks and church plates. I saw angels last night. I seen men with teeth like coins."

"Fuck!" Dottie stared at Claudia through the kitchen window. "He's nuts! Gonna kill us all!"

Ray jabbed the pistol toward the tree line, then swung it back across the porch as if he could see faces in the air.

"Claudia, you think you better than me? Sheriff Harlow, you think I don't remember that stop after Katrina? Y'all all got debts you never paid."

The late-summer heat made tempers short and sweat sting like salt. By Saturday afternoon, Ray was sprawled on the porch, drunker than usual, words slurring into some half-gospel, half-confession. The pistol in his hand wasn't bravado—it was gravity holding a psychotic break in its grasp, and everyone knew it.

Henri drifted back toward the trees after that, leaving the yard to its noise; some work, he knew, didn't belong to witnesses.

Ray waved the gun as he talked, careless, like punctuation, as if the weapon was just another prop in the long sermon of his life. Claudia wiped her hands on her apron and stepped out, voice flat because you don't try altar or argument with a burned-out preacher until you know you have the right prayers. She kept a distance of three porchboards.

"Ray," she said. "Come on. Inside." She thought she'd shepherd him through—like so many other afternoons when he'd cracked open and spilled the heat of his life across the porch.

He laughed, a wet sound, and the pistol came up again.

One of his disgruntled followers picked up a burner phone and called it in. Brother Ray.

The dispatcher wrote it down: male subject, firearm, porch at Bayou House.

• • •

Sheriff Buck came first.

"Ray," he said. "Let's cool off. Talk to me." Ray answered with scripture and bile. Buck tried patience. He radioed in that it was probably nothing, that Ray had a history.

At the third hour he began rattling out old debts, ex-wives, the Army, the Gulf War. He paced the porch, pistol pressed into his palm.

"I'm gonna do it," he said. His voice went small. "I'm gonna blow my head off on this step so they know."

Neighbors gathered. Five hours in, and a cluster had grown into a crowd, phones recording it all.

"He's gonna do it." "Somebody better shoot him first."

A teenage girl held her phone high, livestreaming to a cousin in Mobile; another man muttered about "another Waco in miniature."

A woman tried a brittle laugh. The yard had turned into theater.

Caroline stayed by the doorway through it all, beads moving through her fingers until the skin there went raw, refusing both the crowd and the police anything that looked like consent.

She leaned close to Claudia. "We shoulda sold the house already."

Claudia shook her head, eyes locked on Ray, the red light of Dottie's new camera winking in the eaves. "I don't want to disappear anymore."

She walked out into the yard, beyond the police cordon, a quiet center, watching the man she thought she knew shatter.

The balance finally began to shift. Buck's calm, stretched thin, began to fray.

"Ray," he said. "Put it down, son. It ain't worth a bullet today." The sheriff backed up, measured, deliberate, trying to keep the circle small. He'd seen these things burn out worse than they started, and he wanted no part of that.

• • •

By late afternoon the state trucks rolled in. The men who spilled out were armored and hungry, jacked on adrenaline, and eager to play with their toys.

Frankie had already pulled back; Lila too. Some kinds of attention ruined cases, and this had become one of them.

"You see him waving that piece around?" one muttered, grinning expectantly.

"Known felon with a gun—green light," another said.

"Easy bag. In and out."

"First one through buys the beers tonight."

Another spat into the gravel. "Bet he's got a meth lab under there. We'll light this place up."

One of Dottie's cameras tracked the black trucks across the road in the Dollar General lot. Caroline crossed herself. Claudia tightened her grip on the porch rail.

Policing reduced Ray to a problem set, and the tools they brought were the wrong ones for a man whose enemy was inside his skull.

Ray—drunk, sweating, crying in circles inside—wasn't a threat to anyone but himself. But through the lens of the state, he became a scenario, a live-fire exercise, a problem to be solved with flashbangs and gas.

They set their perimeter like a siege line, all war-footing and bravado, and the neighborhood watched a pathetic, broken man turned into an enemy combatant by sheer appetite for battle.

Ray retreated into the small rooms of the house like someone stepping into a dream that had teeth. He took Claudia's old quilt and looped it around his shoulders and carried the pistol like something that had always been his right hand. He shouted at shadows and named every betrayal. "You won't take what's mine!" he cried, voice cracking, and then quieter, pleading: "Don't make them shoot me. Don't make them take my soul." He walked from the porch to the parlor, then to the kitchen, then back again—a circular liturgy. He threatened to kill himself not as bluster but as a litany. Each threat inched the day toward geometries of danger.

The tactical commander set the perimeter that ate up the block. "We don't need this much show for one drunk with a pistol."

Armored vehicles crouched like beetles in the Dollar General lot. A loudspeaker appeared, making the day reverberate like a turned-over jar. "This is the state police," a recorded voice said. "Ray Daniels, come to the front door. Put down any weapons. We want to help you." The voice was paper-thin over the humidity.

Drones whined overhead. New toys. Negotiators tried mirrors of empathy that bounced off Ray's rage. They offered cigarettes, they offered family voices piped through a radio, they promised that no one wanted him dead. He told the negotiator that promises were like paper—not worth the wet that dissolves them—and he smashed a window, glass fracturing into teeth. The sound of breaking glass was a key in the chest. Moths exploded like ash.

Tear gas came later. A canister arced, then another, and then the inhaled cough that comes with CS intent on clearing a room. Windows were smashed to make space for ventilation; policemen in heavy armor filed through the door like a tide.

The first window shattered shards across the parlor. Another window burst in the dining room, splintering the china cabinet.

On the porch, antique chairs were kicked aside, wicker snapping. Claudia remembered her father falling asleep in one after Sunday dinners, pipe still in his hand, and the laughter of cousins playing tag around his legs.

Tear gas rolled in behind the shattering, yellow smoke curling over photographs and quilts, erasing decades in minutes. To Claudia it felt less like law and more like a sacking—thugs disguised as police, breaking not just a house but the family stitched into every nail and board.

From the yard, Claudia felt the gas creep into her lungs too, a sour bite that made her chest seize. The house itself seemed to choke, walls shuddering with each cough Ray loosed inside. She clutched the porch rail as if her grip could steady the whole structure against its own suffocation.

Ray's hands rose in a half-bent benediction. "Let it burn," he rasped. When the gas hit him he coughed like he was passing through a fever. He staggered, eyes wide and glassy, and when the men in black reached him they moved with a forced gentleness that felt foreign, as if their rifles had hands they were not permitted to use. He threatened, he pleaded, he laughed in a small, insane way that is not laughter at all. A flashbang went off in the kitchen: searing white noise, a concussion that unclipped memory for half a second. The house flinched and sobbed; the rafters sighed like old men waking from a nightmare.

Across the road the crowd had thinned, but those who remained wore the look of parishioners who had stayed too long at a funeral. A boy whispered, "They'll shoot him now, watch." His mother slapped the back of his head, not for the words but for speaking them aloud. Another man filmed through the crack of his truck window, the engine idling like he might need to peel off at any second. Every face was pale with the same mix of horror and hunger: they couldn't look away.

• • •

Claudia watched it all with a clarity that cut tender. She had been through Ray's halting confessions, the cheap redemption he distributed in slugs, but this—this was a fracture. A sheriff's deputy stopped her. "Ma'am, you need to step back," he said.

"This is my house," she said. "You're breaking my house."

Hour seven folded like a bad prayer. The paperwork that tends to follow such days started its quiet work. Someone called legal.

"Dropping these charges," someone said. "Tonight's, anyway."

The arithmetic of influence and money crept in—a friend from the bank, a cousin with a badge, a voice that can make a small town tilt on its axis. Ray still seemed to have some evangelical connections—apparently worth more than Claudia.

There were specifics, always. A banker dialing his brother-in-law in Jackson, who whispered into the ear of a state prosecutor. A sheriff's cousin who carried a badge in Biloxi leaning just enough to make a judge fold the file. Nothing written down, everything understood. Ray's arrest blurred at the edges—charged, then uncharged; detained, then released. His name a passing fog in the clerk's log.

• • •

In the aftermath, the house wheezed. Its porch was splinters.

Ray left in a borrowed shirt, his eyes burned raw and not yet holding the shape of anything. He walked out because somebody had placed a softer hand on a harder ledger, and some sway had convinced a judge or a prosecutor or a sheriff's friend to fold closed the problems that looked like they might make trouble. He wandered the block in the hours after, a figure stitched back together with thread from other people's lives.

A separate hold would soon envelope Ray—old charges, new leverage—and he was quietly rebooked. Not for the siege. The system knew that had been excessive force. But they could still nail Ray for old stuff already waiting in the system. It was time to shut down his light.

Claudia sat on the steps that evening, after they let him go. Ray came and sat four boards away, not speaking.

A truck slowed as it passed, driver's eyes fixed forward, refusing to glance at the wrecked house. Curtains twitched across the street. The whole block seemed to agree on one thing: watch, but don't be seen watching. For a long time they watched a slow, bruised sun die behind the trees, and for a long time there was no sermon, only a shared exhaustion.

By Monday morning the courthouse log in Jackson showed the arrest, then one particular line scratched clean, as if it had never existed. Erased, but not undone.

Other charges remained pending, and now Ray remained in lockup. Not even Pastor Reese or Margaret Ann Whitfield came forward to post his bond—the loyalists who once smoothed things over kept their wallets shut.

Later, a clerk would mutter about a late-night call from the Attorney General's office, the kind that arrived without explanation and ended with silence. In Biloxi, a cousin with a badge joked darkly over coffee that paper burns fast if you know where to hold the match. Claudia did not feel relief. That night she woke choking. Every slammed car door sent her bolt upright.

No one came by. Not the neighbors who had filled their phones with footage, not the congregation that once claimed her family as their own. Only her four sisters knocked, bringing food and soft words, circling her like a guardrail against the emptiness. The rest of the town passed her on the sidewalk with eyes fixed ahead, pretending not to see.

Caroline lingered last, setting her beads on the counter. "We can't live like this, Claudie. The house is killing us."

Claudia checked the memory card from Dottie's porch cam, the red light still blinking steady. "Or it's keeping us alive."

Claudia already registered that her footage might outlast the official narrative. It might just be the pocket rocket—the thing that stayed lit after everything else burned—that would save Ray.

For the first time, Caroline didn't answer. Silence between them felt sharper than any sermon. Claudia understood then that Bayou House would never be rebuilt in the context of community—it was hers and

Caroline's alone to inhabit, theirs alone to remember, theirs alone to carry now in nightmares.

Twenty-One
DOUBLING DOWN

Ray walked out of county lockup on a Tuesday, bailed by a bondsman fronted by a Gulfport LLC. He stepped into daylight with the smirk of a man who believed himself too slick for consequence. Claudia had waited for a call.

The only story that carried was Ray's lie that she had called in the SWAT team—on her own house. Then he salted the lie all over town.

By Friday night the First Baptist fellowship hall was vibrating like a campaign rally. The cinderblock walls were strung with streamers in purple and gold. Folding tables sagged under crockpots of gumbo and chili, aluminum trays of cornbread, and sheet cakes piped with Bible verses.

Claudia took the back row. From there she had the whole view—shoulders hunched, rings clinking against cups, eyes darting. Dottie had told her to go alone. Fewer faces, less noise. It was one moment Claudia hadn't asked the others to sit through.

"The world may accuse," Pastor Reese thundered from a podium. He dabbed his forehead with a handkerchief. "But the Spirit redeems. Tonight we stand with Brother Ray, a man who has walked through fire and come out anointed."

The applause swelled. They brought Ray forward like a prizefighter in a borrowed blazer, sleeves too long, grin wolfish.

He took the microphone. "I was a man in the pit," he drawled like it was a tent revival. "But the Lord—through you—pulled me out.

Don't let the liars and the haters stop what the Lord has begun."

The crowd roared. Hands rose. The offering baskets began their rounds, soon bursting with cash envelopes and checks. Claudia let the noise wash over her and began her own accounting instead.

Claudia catalogued names. Margaret Ann Whitfield was there, her diamond bracelets glittering. Mayor Hal Holcomb huddled with a bank vice president, each scribbling notes without glancing down.

It wasn't charity. It was laundering. Claudia knew their nonprofit 990s. Budgets bloated with "community programming." Half a million for "rehabilitation services." Another quarter million for "partnership outreach." Even more routed through real estate—charity thrift stores opened in boarded-up strip centers, money passing clean on paper and dirty everywhere else.

The money flowed back to its source: cousins on nonprofit boards. Fraternity brothers as "consultants." A cottage industry of redemption-for-hire.

Behind Claudia, whispers: "Such courage, to come back after all he's been through."

"He's proof the system works—we give, the Lord blesses."

They weren't applauding Ray. They were applauding their own absolution.

She almost rose, almost loosed the fire in her throat: What about what he's already done? To me. To my family. To the women he's bled dry? But her fury found no landing, smothered by Styrofoam cups and pious nods.

Ray raised his hands. "The Bayou Brotherhood is more than a ministry now. It's a movement. Don't let the lies stop what the Lord has begun."

The applause grew louder, suffocating thought itself. The 'Goula Gospel had always worked this way.

Then he leaned in. "You know the story of Delilah. She thought she could cut down the man of God. But the Lord—He turned even that for His glory."

He hadn't named Claudia. He didn't need to.

Claudia pressed her pen with more names until the paper shredded.

He was theirs now, a vessel for their guilt-washed grace. She traced every hand that signed, every bowed head, every smirk of self-regard. It was a pipeline: old money, new money, plantation families and bankers laundering their legacies through casseroles and hymnals. Not saving— shielding.

She knew the system now, and still its normalcy shocked her. Wash your hands in donations and call them clean.

What they were celebrating had names she carried. Claudia knew the other ledger well. The women who skipped the park after dusk because Ray's men had claimed it. The single mom whose food stamps vanished into beer and smokes. The shelters and laundromats taxed by street enforcers. The quiet terror of families barely surviving, painted as the problem, while Ray's flock paraded as trophies.

None of that made it to the sanctuary lights. What shone there was redemption cheap as raffle tickets, so long as you signed your name.

Ray lifted his arms, the congregation roaring like they'd seen a miracle. At first his words rolled the way they always had—pit to pulpit, sin to salvation. Then he slowed, voice dropping to that husky register he used when he wanted to plant a hook.

"There's always someone," he said, "waiting with the scissors. Someone who thinks they can cut down what God Himself has raised up. But the Lord turns even betrayal into blessing. The righteous cannot be bound."

The crowd murmured their amens, hungry for the parable. Every eye slid sideways in her direction. She met their looks with utter defiance.

Twenty-Two
THE JULEP ROOM

Ray came back harder, louder. Jail hadn't broken him—it had armed him. In his telling, he hadn't been arrested for terrorizing his own household; he'd been tried by darkness and returned with testimony. He called the sheriff Pilate, hinted at a woman with scissors in the night, and lifted his mother to the stature of Mary, long-suffering and misunderstood. He stacked his suffering on top of theirs until the story of Christ bent into his own reflection.

"You're either with me and God, or against us," he told a handful of strays.

They weren't much—three men with sagging jeans and ankle monitors, two women with baby strollers parked at the back wall of the hall—but in Ray's mind, they were the remnant. The faithful. His proof that the world couldn't starve him of an audience.

Then came the new girlfriend. She was blonde and thin. Someone he could control. She worked days at a nail salon and nights at a check-cashing place, but somehow she scraped together enough to buy him a car—a used Buick the color of tarnished brass, seats worn thin but engine steady. Ray called it an "offering to God's work," though the title sat in her name. "The Lord moves through His people," he told her, pressing his hand on her forehead as though he were blessing her with tongues. She shook like a tuning fork.

By Sunday, he was parading it down Government Street, windows down, gospel so loud windows rattled. He leaned out the driver's side with one arm stretched like a conquering general, shouting scripture at pedestrians who barely looked up. "The enemy cannot stop us! The enemy cannot stop us!" Every red light became a pulpit.

By Tuesday, he was preaching about rebuilding his family. Not the one that knew his temper and left, not the daughters and ex-wives scattered like seeds in soil too poor to grow, but a manufactured family, forged by fire and obedience. He said blood wasn't thicker than spirit, that loyalty to him was loyalty to God. He began drawing charts on poster board—circles and arrows showing who would answer to whom, how the money would flow.

He talked about housing them together in trailers, a "compound" where he could shepherd the flock without interference. He declared that anyone who questioned his authority would be "cast out into the wilderness." He didn't say power; he said protection. Everyone heard power.

By Friday, he walked the perimeter of other people's houses, rattling knobs. He tested locks the way other men tested fences, not quite breaking in but pushing until wood and metal remembered his touch. One neighbor came home early and found Ray standing in her carport, hands folded behind his back like a deacon waiting to be acknowledged. He said he was "praying for her household." She called the sheriff, but by the time the cruiser rolled through, Ray was gone—already back at the fellowship hall, burnishing the Buick with a church rag and telling anyone who would listen that the devil was trying to silence him again.

• • •

Claudia had stopped answering her phone. She stopped answering the door. Jehovah's Witnesses, UPS drivers, neighbors leaving pound cake—she let them all knock until their knuckles gave out. Even the bayou, once her sanctuary, seemed too close, too watchful. Cypress knees looked like teeth waiting to bite, the water a mirror she couldn't bear to face.

The surgery had promised relief. Instead, the wound closed, but nerves burned, fingers stiffened. Pain moved through her like weather fronts, sudden and merciless, and nothing stilled it. The doctor called it a suboptimal outcome. She called it a hex she didn't believe in.

She wrapped herself in blankets and shadows, shuffling between the couch and the bed, measuring time by the rise and fall of her pain pills. Days spilled like water with no rim, dissolving into each other. She forgot to eat, then ate too much, then forgot again. Coffee sat cold in mugs, the surface slick with oil like the top of a swamp. Mold crept on dishes she couldn't bring herself to wash. Laundry slumped in piles, clothes smelling of damp earth.

The television murmured endlessly in the background, voices talking at her, through her, around her. She wasn't really watching; she was hiding in the noise. The sound of her own silence had become unbearable. At night she kept the volume low enough to drown the creak of the floorboards but high enough to remind her she wasn't alone.

Commercials became lullabies; laugh tracks, alarms.

Caroline found her there one afternoon, blinds drawn, air stale with damp fabric and uneaten food. She didn't knock this time—just came in with a key she wasn't supposed to have, her jaw set tight as barbed wire.

"Look at you," she said, standing over Claudia like she couldn't believe the ruin in front of her. "He did this to you. Ray did this. To you, to me, to Bayou House. He poisoned everything."

Claudia tried to pull the blanket over her face, but her arm spasmed and she winced.

Tears came hot and unbidden.

"Don't you dare cry for him," Caroline snapped. "That man crucified you and called it love. He burned your house down in spirit before he ever tried to break in. He doesn't deserve your tears."

Claudia sobbed harder. "But what if I love him," she whispered.

Caroline's face twisted, grief and fury tangling into something raw. "Oh for fuck's sake! After what he's done? After what he's still doing? Christ, Claudia. He'll kill you.

"He'll kill us all if you keep holding onto him like he's the only man God ever made."

Silence fell between them, jagged as glass. Claudia's chest heaved, her arm jerked with pain, and she turned her wet face toward Caroline.

"Fuck off," she said hoarsely. "Just…fuck off and leave me alone."

Caroline's eyes flickered—hurt, then steel. She dropped the blanket she'd been about to pull around Claudia, turned on her heel, and slammed the door so hard the picture frames rattled. Claudia was left alone in the dim, wrapped in a house that now sounded like it breathed without her.

• • •

PTSD wasn't a diagnosis—it became Claudia's diet. Her thoughts chewed her from the inside out. Every knock at the door replayed the memory of boots on her mother's porch. Every car engine idling outside was Ray's, even if the headlights never swept her windows. Her chest tightened when the wind rattled the siding, when a dog barked two houses over, when kids shrieked in play on the street. Everything sounded like warning.

The grocery store, the post office, even the front yard—off-limits. The one time she tried, just to check the mailbox, her knees buckled halfway down the walk. She clawed her way back to the doorframe, sweating, dizzy, hearing her pulse roar like a siren in her ears. After that she let the envelopes pile, their edges curling from the damp.

When she dreamed, she dreamed of locks snapping open, of Ray's voice pouring through the house like gas waiting for a match. When she woke, her arm spasmed so hard she bit her tongue. She learned to taste iron and keep breathing. The pain kept her grounded. The fear kept her alive.

• • •

It was three days later when Caroline stopped waiting for her sister to snap out of it. She swung her beat-up Cadillac Seville into the gravel lot of Aunt Jenny's Catfish Parlor, tires crunching as the headlights cut across the old clapboard building. The place sat heavy against the trees, veranda sagging with age, as though it had been listening in on Ocean Springs gossip for a century and had grown tired of carrying the weight. She killed the engine beneath a stand of dripping live oaks, chrome flashing once before the car went dark.

Moments later, Dottie's Dodge Ram pulled in beside her, coughing smoke, with Lila and Frankie climbing down from the cab.

You found the bar by going down—not just the stairs beneath Aunt Jenny's Catfish Parlor, but down through temperature and pressure. Upstairs: grease, chatter, fry oil popping. Down here: cool air, damp brick, the low hum of something older than music.

The bricks were rolled clay, fired two centuries ago, sweating through Gulf Coast humidity. You could feel it if you leaned close—cool moisture on your knuckles, like the room was breathing. Locals said the walls remembered more than catfish and cocktails. Nobody laughed when they said it.

Some claimed the cellar had started as a storm shelter, dug deep in the 1800s to ride out hurricanes and hide from Union patrols. Others went darker. Before the restaurant, before the house above it was respectable, the basement had been a place for people no one wanted—madmen, runaways, women who wouldn't behave. No records ever surfaced, but the story never died. The mortar held it. You could feel it when the room went quiet.

By the time the girls slid into the Julep that night, it was dressed in its mid-century skin. Elvis posters curled slightly at the edges, cheap reproductions but placed with care—'56, '57, his clean-cut years on the Gulf Coast, hiding out with his girlfriend, June Jaunico. He'd park his pink Cadillac where Caroline had parked hers, and they'd sneak downstairs for mint juleps without bourbon. He didn't drink then.

The corner booth was still scarred enough that people argued whether his initials had ever been there at all. Dottie still loved the place. She'd bartended here years before, and liked to show off a small shrine to Billie Holiday—black-and-white photos, a cracked album sleeve framed crooked, a cigarette burn in the rail that no amount of polishing had ever lifted.

The ceiling was low enough to make you aware of your body. Sound stayed contained. Conversations here didn't drift—they settled.

Tourists upstairs ate fried green tomatoes and never suspected a thing. But the Julep wasn't a bar to those who knew it. It was a holding space. A place where past and present rubbed together until something sparked. A room where plans came out sharper than prayers.

That's why they chose it.

The four of them claimed the back corner booth. Caroline slid in first, smoothing her skirt, her eyes sharp. When the bartender drifted over, she didn't hesitate.

"Water Lily," she said, voice crisp. The bartended raised an eyebrow—people usually ordered beer or bourbon here.

"Vodka, simple syrup, crème de violette. Lemon. Heavy on the violette."

"And you ladies?"

Dottie let out a low sneer, gravel turning in her throat. "Christ, Caroline. Save the garden for church teas. Two Buds in a bottle."

Lila tugged her cardigan tighter. "Orange Fanta," she said softly. The bartender nodded and walked off.

Caroline broke the silence first, exhaling a sharp plume of smoke. "We can't keep circling the drain with her. Ray's building an army and Claudia's rotting in that house. He wins both ways if we don't move."

"I can't belief she let him come back to the fucking garage," Lila replied.

Dottie patted her arm. "I've done worse for a man I loved, Lila."

"He doesn't love her," Caroline said. "Narcissists never do."

Dottie leaned forward, elbows heavy on the table. "So what—you want us to march into his new compound? Preach at him until he lays down the sword?" She snorted. "He'll laugh in our faces. Or worse."

"That man ain't laughing," Frankie said, voice low, steady. "He's recruiting. Charts and rules like he's Moses come down the mountain. He wants obedience. He wants her as the prize—proof he can still break what's unbroken."

"Naah, he wants Bayou House. So he can set up his fucking commune," Dottie growled.

Lila shifted, condensation dripping onto her hand. "Claudia still loves him," she said, almost apologetically. "I heard her say it. You can't just tear that out of her chest with force."

"Love?" Caroline snapped. "Love is what's killing her. She's chained to the memory of a man who doesn't exist. The man she wants is the sermon he tells about himself."

The waitress dropped off their drinks and hurried away. Caroline took a long sip of the violet cocktail, lips stained faint purple. She set the glass down hard.

"So here's what we do," she said. "We make it impossible for him to touch her. If she won't save herself, we wall her off with something stronger than locks and pity."

"And we got the Toussaints," Lila continued. "Let's ask them to cook the strongest keeping work they trust—not curses. Something that burns if he even breathes near her door."

Dottie snorted. "I don't trust half the hocus-pocus they sell, but I'll take a bag that stinks enough to keep him from crossing a threshold. Man like Ray don't fear cops—he fears what he can't name."

"And Frankie," Caroline continued, "we need proof—paper, receipts, anything. He's skimming cash through that so-called ministry. If we put the right trail in the sheriff's hands, Ray doesn't just look crazy—he looks criminal."

Frankie leaned back, chewing her thumbnail. "I'll start with the deposits. He always dodges the ten-grand threshold—$9,980 like a tick. That's his tell. I'll stack the slips until the sheriff has to notice."

"And Lila," Caroline said more gently, "you're the only one she'll still let in. Slide the gris-gris into her pocket. Keep her anchored, no matter how much she swears she wants him. If she tries to push you out, push back harder."

Lila's eyes flicked to the jukebox. "She doesn't need sermons. She needs someone to eat cold cereal with. I can do that. Anchor first, advice never."

The jukebox crackled—a bar of some old Elvis tune—then cut dead again. The four women listened to the silence swallow it.

Caroline tapped ash into the tray, voice low but razor-sharp. "He thinks he's untouchable. We're not waiting for him to knock down her door. We move first. This time, it's our war."

Something in Caroline's face softened, a private weather that made the others look up.

"Claudia's my sister. Older by twelve minutes. She used to steal my socks and tuck them under her pillow so the tooth fairy couldn't find them. She's always been the brave one. Now she needs me."

Her hand went to the scar at the base of her thumb, the one from the railway bridge dare when they were seven.

"She's always been the brave one. Now she's the one with a tremor. She's the one who needs me."

The women let her words hang there. They understood completely.

Caroline's voice hardened back into steel. "I don't care if it's love or memory or whatever ghost is propping her up. I'm not letting him make her a sacrifice. Not on my watch."

Dottie slammed her beer and the booth jumped. "Then we do it clean. No heroics that get us jailed or dead." Her voice landed like a gavel. She looked at each woman in turn, naming them like ingredients in a working.

"Toussaints give us cover—gris-gris stitched with salt and bone-smoke. Not for curses, for keeping. A line that says: this far and no farther."

She turned to Frankie. "You find the money trail. That's your spell. Every tithe, every jar, every receipt he's too sloppy to hide. Paper is power. Pin him down with his own handwriting."

Her gaze landed on Lila, softer. "You be Claudia's shadow. Sit with her. Love held steady is the strongest mojo."

Then she jabbed her thumb at Caroline. "And you. You want him out of her head? Be the front. Make him stumble in public, where he can't rewrite the story. Drag the man out from under his miracle."

The plan hung in the air like smoke. Four of them binding themselves to action, each role a charm, each step practical "magic" that would still hold up in court.

Caroline's jaw set. "I'll do it loud and ugly if I have to. I'll make him perform in front of witnesses until he trips on his own sermon." She smiled then, small and dangerous. "But first: we stitch Claudia into something she can hold onto. Nothing mystical—just a line to the ground. A schedule. Meals. A face at the door that's not his."

Frankie—quiet until now—nodded. "I can get receipts. I can follow money. Ray's sloppy when he thinks he's sacred." She bit the inside of her cheek. "There's a county clerk who hates him for how he treated her nephew. I think she'll talk."

Lila's fingers trembled on her glass, then steadied. "I'll be there," she said. "Every Sunday if she lets me. If she says she wants him, I'll sit with her while she says it. I won't argue. I'll just be there."

They drew the plan in shorthand, no grand speeches—keeping bag, receipts, lunchtime calls, a doctor on retainer, a get-out bag in Dottie's truck. Practicalities, then teeth. Caroline finished, voice thinner now, private and fierce: "You were always brave,

Claud. I'll be the noise until you can be the nerve."

A silence followed, not the empty kind but the kind that holds oaths. Caroline tilted her glass to Dottie's bottle, Frankie gave a shadow of a nod, Lila's soda fizzed like a yes.

It wasn't a prayer, but it bound like one.

The jukebox coughed again, a muted blues riff that wandered off into nothing.

Outside, a warm September rain began in a long, patient hiss against the clapboard.

They rose together, sleeves tugged down against the draft, and went back out into the lot—four women with a plan, and a sister waiting in a house that had forgotten how to breathe.

Twenty-Three
STING

Frankie sat on her porch. Her beer had gone warm. She set it on the rail and opened the box on the table she'd been feeding for months: receipts, $9,980 deposits, bank slips, cash-app screenshots. Vendor invoices from "Bayou Brotherhood" to companies with matching surnames. A property title tying the parsonage to a shell company in Gulfport.

She worked best when the mess became a system. If Ray and all the godfearing men and women hiding behind their sermons were going to go down, it would be on paper. There were gate logs in the box. Receipts. Dates, plate numbers, timestamped roll-ups. Ray's Buick, three of his lieutenants, the banker's Escalade, all within the same 47-minute deposit window.

Then the minutes. Frankie flipped through church board notes, photocopied by a secretary who thought Jesus would want transparency. "Emergency allocation to Brotherhood—$42,500." Line after line with "community impact" as the fig leaf.

Frankie texted the group, because she didn't bother calling. This was logistics, not comfort. Texts left a trail she could screenshot, timestamp, and hand to a judge if she had to.

> Frankie: "Time for our little treasure chest. We got the receipts."
> Dottie: "Treasure chest???"
> Frankie: "We rent a vault…as a prop."
> Caroline: "Oooooo. Go on."
> Frankie: "We stage the reveal at their revival."
> Lila: "Oh shit. I like it. They think it's money. It's all the evidence."

Dottie: "Fucking genius. Let's do it."
Frankie: "They want a circus, we'll give 'em Barnum. Legally, though."

At a pre-dawn meeting at the courthouse annex, Frankie laid out the evidence—tabs for DEPOSITS, VENDORS, GATE LOGS, PROPERTY, COMMS—to the Assistant District Attorney.

"We're not arresting anybody on a stage," the ADA said. "That's not how we do things around here."

"Don't need you to," Frankie said. "We need service. Subpoenas for the bank, storage unit, the benevolence account. Warrants later if the math holds."

At the courthouse, Caroline sat down with Sheriff Buck. He studied the gate logs, the structuring pattern, the "consultant" checks to cousins. "You planning a show?" he asked.

Caroline smiled. "You could say that."

They set a date. Service at 7:00 p.m., during a planned Brotherhood rally in the First Baptist fellowship hall. Not a raid—notice. Deputies were already fanning out quietly: two at the church with subpoenas, two at Coast Storage to freeze the lockers named in Frankie's tabs, one at the banker's office with a records subpoena. If anyone showed up armed at the revival, that would be its own separate charge. But the point wasn't cuffs. The point was exposure.

Caroline booked the same fellowship hall for "A Night of Testimony," rented a floor safe and printed foam-board blowups of the cleanest slips. She also ordered a vinyl banner that read RECEIPTS, NOT RUMORS. They were going to crash Pastor Reese's party.

Lila called the local paper—a features reporter with a nose for civic theater—and tipped her off to "a community truth-telling."

Claudia, at Caroline's insistence, left town that afternoon. If the night went sideways, she'd be clean. She protested—weakly at first, then exhausted by pain and dread—then went. She wanted absolution; distance was step one.

• • •

They loaded the vault through the church's kitchen door an hour before the rally. Dottie rolled the safe like a funeral director with a stubborn casket. Frankie set the easels beneath the buzzing fluorescents, laid out the binders with tabs like teeth. Lila taped subpoenas to clipboards, each one flagged for a deputy. Caroline fussed with sightlines until the room felt like a courtroom.

At seven, the congregation arrived. Ray strutted late, Bible in one hand. He looked at the safe, the banners, the news camera, and grinned.

Pastor Reese opened with a prayer. Sheriff's deputies took positions near the side doors.

Ray took the mic. "We're here tonight," he said, "because the enemy can't stand a work of God."

"They can try to bury us," he said as he gestured toward the safe. "But they didn't know we were seeds."

"Brother Ray," Caroline called from the back. "Let's open it together. Receipts, not rumors." A murmur ran the walls. Ray waved her forward. Frankie, Dottie, and Lila joined her as Ray started looking pale.

Dottie popped the safe. Inside: binders and foam-boards. Caroline lifted the first blowup—a casino deposit slip for $9,980, the bank's timestamp matching perfectly.

"This is from two days after the 'widows and orphans' drive," she said. "Nine deposits in three weeks, all just shy of a federal report. That's structuring."

She slid it onto an easel.

The second: a vendor invoice to MAGNOLIA CROWN CONSULTING, address matching a deacon's hunting camp. The third: a property title deeded out, then leased back at four times market.

Ray laughed. "You don't know what you're looking at, sister," he said. "Those are tools of ministry."

"You're a fraud," someone shouted from the side wall.

"Tools of ministry?" another voice laughed, sharp and humorless. "Whose ministry?"

"Not mine."

"Where's our money?"

Frankie handed a reporter a packet. "Here's the ministry," she said. "Page twelve is Ray and Pastor Reese's parsonage lease. Page twenty shows where they run their poker nights. Page twenty-seven has the gate logs—with license plates of many of these fine folks here tonight—arriving within the hour of deposits."

Ray reached under the podium and pulled free a bullhorn.

A deputy stepped to the mic. "We're serving subpoenas for records," he said. "To the bank, the storage facility, to Bayou Brotherhood Ministries. No one is under arrest for now. That's all."

He walked the paperwork to Ray, Pastor Reese, the church treasurer.

Ray blanched, looking to Pastor Reese for reassurance. There was none.

"This is a smear," he shouted into the bullhorn. Every head in the crowd started wagging as people began to leave.

The show was over.

Ray tried to hand the papers back. The deputy set them on the podium and walked away.

Caroline raised the fourth board: a hand-annotated ledger from a church elder's laptop—a copy obtained by subpoena when the elder's son, tired of threats, swore an affidavit. Lines of "benevolence" outflows marched to cousins' LLCs, to "consultants," to cashier's checks paid to "R. Reese"—Ray's alias of convenience—the line item OUTREACH written beside each.

Gasps turned to a hush that felt heavier than anger. Fear of exposure changed the air pressure. Frankie watched the faces harden and pale and felt the first twist of it in her gut—not triumph, not mercy, just math landing where faith used to sit.

You could feel the congregation recalculating: How close am I to this? Do my checks show?

Ray reached under the podium and pulled free a bullhorn. "Lies, all of it," he shouted over the microphone's feedback. "Enemies at the gate! Wolves in ribbons!"

Two of his men edged toward the front—one with a clip-knife on his belt, another with a pistol grip printing under his hoodie. A deputy peeled from the wall, eyes on hands.

"Sir," he said to the first, "knife on church property violates your parole. Hands where I can see them."

The man balked, then froze as the second deputy stepped in. It wasn't theater; it was plain law. The knife went into an evidence bag. The man was escorted out—not slammed—booked on a parole violation at the curb. The second, with an outstanding failure-to-appear on a theft case, went quietly when they confirmed his warrant by radio.

No one put cuffs on Ray. Not yet. The vault had done its work. Lila, standing near mothers with strollers, spoke without raising her voice. "You told us receipts, not rumors," she said to the room.

"Now we have them." She looked at the reporter. "You wanted a quote? Write that."

The reporter's camera caught the foam-boards, the served subpoenas, the sheriffs walking out two men without spectacle. She already had on-the-record confirmation from the ADA that "evidence of possible structuring and self-dealing" was under review.

Ray turned on Caroline, then on Frankie, searching for a bullet to fire. "You think this ends me?" he shouted. "You think you can stop the hand of God?"

Caroline didn't flinch. "Paper is how you paid yourself. Paper is how we stop you."

He dropped the bullhorn, gathered the subpoenas, and walked out with three reporters hot on his heels.

• • •

The arrests that night were for a parole violation, an outstanding warrant for failure-to-appear, and a citation for disorderly conduct when a cousin tried to shoulder a deputy.

By morning, subpoenas had frozen storage units, church accounts, title companies, and lawyers' offices. Bank compliance officers were lawyering up. One church treasurer, pale as the sheet cake, called an emergency meeting and then his own lawyer.

The Magnolia Crown casino was suddenly raided by U.S. marshals.

The web that held Ocean Springs together—IOUs, benevolence envelopes, handshake loans labeled "missions"—tightened, then snapped. The soup kitchen turned away seconds. A motel clerk who'd been floating families on quiet twenties stopped, hands shaking over the till. Casino markers, once covered by anonymous "donations," came due in hard light.

Ray's remnant felt it like a stomach flu. The martyr story soured; the math didn't. A man who'd sworn fealty at every altar call stared at his name on a copy of a gate log and couldn't make it holy. Another smashed a truck window behind the pawn shop and stood still while a bored patrolman wrote him up. Loyalty, it turned out, was a currency with a receipt.

Frankie's victory tasted like iron. She'd wanted him stopped, not starved, but paper starves loud men. She slept two hours, woke, checked the ADA's email—acknowledged receipt, next steps, no promises. She stared at the photo in the Sun Herald: Caroline holding a foam-board like a shield; Lila with a hand on a mother's shoulder; Dottie in the corner, arms crossed, looking like the patron saint of "try me."

Dottie was already on step two, a quiet spreadsheet with names redacted and chains of custody documented, in case the sheriff tried to "lose" anything. She called the bondsman anyway, not for Ray but for the two dumb cousins—"Everyone gets a lawyer," she said, "even when they're fools."

Lila burned the last of a church-safe candle on her porch and watched the smoke climb.

"He'll come back," she said. It wasn't dread. It was a forecast.

They did find a scrap later that night, not a blood promise in the marsh but a torn corner of a foam-board, tire-scuffed and damp near the fellowship hall's side door…NOT RUMORS.

Someone slid it into a manila envelope and tucked it into Frankie's box. Evidence of a different kind—the kind that proved the room had existed.

The town rearranged itself after their sting. Several pulpits stood empty for a few weeks before visiting preachers started going with homilies about forgiveness that sounded small.

In Gulf Shores, Claudia watched the coverage roll in on mute. The captions crawled beneath Ray's face—STRUCTURING, SUBPOENAS, SELF-DEALING—and she realized she was breathing without counting again. Her arm still hurt. The fear hadn't left. But the noise had shifted away from her door.

She walked out on the balcony and continued reading the articles. She texted Caroline: "Wow." Then another: "Thanks."

In the following weeks, rumors ran like electricity. Old friends and churchgoers avoided eye contact in the produce aisle. One bank manager took a month of personal days. A deacon resigned "to spend more time with his family," and the chamber of commerce canceled several luncheons with no explanation.

Ray would be back. Many would scurry. A few might leave town entirely hoping to avoid indictment. Others with debts they could no longer pay knew they risked becoming gator bait if they didn't make things right.

It would be a slow tidal surge that could no longer be sandbagged with sermons.

Twenty-Four
COPPER BOWLS

Henri arrived first, a bundle under his arm and a small copper bowl. Behind him came Yvette and Lila with baskets of crushed resins and a paper sack of pepper.

They walked the yard then slowly drew a border. Lila pinched cayenne and sifted a red line across the threshold. Henri followed with cornmeal, laying vevè on the warped porch.

Incense swelled sweet and sharp. The copper bowl glowed and spit light. Henri found his first heartbeats on his Djembe drum, wrists loose, shoulders easy. Nothing spooky.

Word of their sting ricocheted all over town, from fellowship halls to gas pumps, shrimp docks, and small kitchens.

"It's all there on paper," someone said at the Family Dollar. "Cash pulls. Cage slips. Fraud. Liars and cheats."

Claudia heard the news on her porch—Lila on speaker—a little angry she'd been benched.

"You went and did it without me," she said, and there was a sting to it, a salt she didn't want to hide. "Fine. But you bring me the receipts."

They did. By nightfall the kitchen table was covered. Dottie had her legal pad and a binder fat with copies; Frankie had sticky notes. Lila set a baby-blue tape recorder on top of a stack of envelopes.

Dottie read in a voice that made even lies sit up straighter. "IOUs signed. 'Benevolence Fund'—Ray's—with no ledger match. Drawer discrepancies, twelve nights running. 9,980—again and again—Magnolia Crown, Sandbar Belle."

She tapped a slip twice with her pen. "This one's stamped October 12."

Frankie traced arrows on the paper. "Benevolence fund to BBM," she said. "BBM to consult fee on the McKinnon flip. Consult fee out to cash, cash to cage, cage back to benevolence. That's the circle. Round and round until even the God talk goes dizzy." She slid the map forward. "Documents outlive charisma every time."

Outside, word kept moving. In the church lot a handful of Ray's faithful traded cigarettes and scripture and tried to square their pastor's voice with the math. Some went home. Some got louder. The fellowship hall doors slammed and opened and slammed again, the echo repeating until even the night got tired of it.

Henri's drum built without hurry, one beat settling into the next, until they were speaking in a rhythm everyone already knew. His hands were patient. Yvette kept to the steps, lips moving in a prayer no one else knew, eyes never leaving the line she and her husband had drawn.

Lila stood at the pepper line like a warden and a mother, letting the smoke curl up and bless her face.

They felt him before they saw him.

Ray stepped out of the darkness.

The porch went still.

He stopped at the edge of the yard and tried a smile.

"Claudie," he said, voice dipped in honey. "They're telling lies about me."

"We got paper," Claudia said. She stood in the doorframe behind Yvette's cayenne line. "Paper doesn't lie the way you do."

Ray laughed. "I know who called the dogs. But I'm a forgiving man, you know that. God's got a plan here, and we—"

"Stop," she said.

Caroline stood behind her, one hand on the doorframe.

He leaned toward the pepper line like he might step across if he could remember how to lift his foot. "I mean it. We can fix this, you and me. You think those girls are your friends, but they're using you for a show. They want to play hero. I'm the only one who ever saw you—"

"I never turned you in," Claudia said. "I never told a cop what you did to me. You don't get to come in my yard and say my name like it's a key. You never owned the lock."

Henri's drum beat echoed. Inside, Dottie and Frankie stayed with the papers, quiet.

"We were good together," he said. "You know we were. You were broken and I… I was building you back."

"You were breaking me," she said, and it wasn't accusation so much as inventory. "You were building yourself a pulpit on my back—and Caroline's, too, with the house—and calling it love."

She took one step forward closer to the red line.

"There's no sermon that makes this right."

He looked past her into the house. Lila moved a half-step behind Claudia and the pepper line flashed red again. "You don't cross this," Lila said. "Be smart, Ray."

He straightened and decided to be righteous. "You think your hedge witches gonna save you? You think your little drum circle changes what God says about authority, about—"

Henri's hands rolled a thunder that shook his words loose and sent them skittering into the grass. The women had come out onto the porch without Claudia noticing. Frankie on the left, Dottie on the right, Lila with a mouthful of pins.

They made a circle because circles hold. Fingers threaded. The drum beat rose to meet them. If there were prayers, they were small ones.

"Let him go from us," Dottie, the skeptic, began. "Let him find a road that doesn't point back,"

Frankie squinted, seeing the map in her head already redrawn without him as the dirty sun in the center. "Let the house keep her," Lila murmured.

Ray took one more step forward and flinched when smoke gusted at his shins. Magic or ash, he felt something that did not welcome him. His eyes flicked to Claudia, looking for something. She offered nothing.

"I'm telling you what I need," she said. "Get the fuck out. Leave Ocean Springs. Don't come back. You keep my name out of your mouth and you stay off this porch. That is the only mercy you get from me."

Caroline smiled at her sister and nodded.

Ray opened his hands like he might offer apology, then closed them when he realized he didn't have one to give.

They each knew he would choose the story that had always loved him best. He shook his head and began to back away slowly.

Henri's drumbeats didn't chase him. They settled. The rich incense thinned.

Claudia watched him vanish. For the first time, the silence didn't scare her.

She crossed the pepper line at threshold and joined the others now seated on the porch. Henri smiled, his drum falling silent as Yvette leaned on his shoulder. No one said anything for a while.

• • •

The news traveled fast. By midmorning folks were saying Brother Ray Broussard had folded and walked away.

"Stepping back to pray," he'd called it, though everyone knew that while he had been a convenient prayer puppet for the Gulf Coast elite, he was likely looking at a criminal indictment too.

Down at the bank, a state monitor's name was added to the Brotherhood's accounts like frost;

Trey Langston stopped pretending the pattern was an accident and cut a deal—structuring, falsified entries, and a promise to talk first thing Monday.

That afternoon, Sheriff Buck was back at Bayou House. He didn't climb the steps at first. He remained in the yard, hat in hand, gravel in his throat.

"Ms. Marston… Ms. Marston!" he said, nodding to each sister. "We served three subpoenas last night. Judge signed off on a temporary order this morning—puts an independent monitor over the Brotherhood's money till the audit's through."

"Pastor Reese?" Caroline asked.

"Resigned before breakfast," Buck said. "Said he was 'stepping back to pray.' He'll be praying with counsel."

"And Trey Langston?" Dottie's voice from the porch, arms crossed.

"Plea deal is on the table—structuring and false filings. He's agreed to cooperate. First appearance Monday."

Claudia kept her eyes on the yard, feeling judgment slowly lift. "And Ray?"

Sheriff Buck's mouth made a thin line. "No arrest—yet. Temporary protective order's active. He violates it, you call me. We'll make that one easy."

He set an envelope on the rail. "Victim services info for ya."

Buck put his hat back, eyes still lowered. He didn't know what else to say, and Claudia was too tired and numb to offer him absolution for what the town had done.

He left.

Caroline peeled open a frost-wrinkled Ziploc and handed it to her sister.

"Got something for you. Remember this?"

It was a single page, yellowed, folded twice— the letter she'd kept on ice in the freezer since the hospital. Their mother's handwriting.

Girls, if the house ever goes dark, don't stare at the dark. Look at the lilies.

Claudia swallowed. "I hear you, Mama," she said. "Let's do it, Caroline."

• • •

The once-powerful in town found petty ways to take control again. Seconds at the soup line stopped. Church charity tightened. Sign-in sheets became wristbands, then QR codes. Pantry boxes got lighter. At the supermarket, people kept their eyes on produce and their mouths shut.

A few days later, the pastor stopped appearing. The auxiliary boards dissolved quietly. The shell charities froze their accounts and came back under new names. The sermons got shorter. The talk about mercy stayed. The talk about money didn't.

On the porch at Bayou House, Dottie watched the street and shrugged, "We did what we could do."

Lila shook her head once. "Now they gotta learn how to act right. How to be neighbors and friends."

Frankie didn't look up from her phone. "Or they'll find a new Ray."

• • •

They had a slumber party that night out on the porch at Bayou House.

"Tonight, and tomorrow, ladies…and gentleman," Dottie laughed, pointing at Henri. "Is party time! You wanna know why?"

"Why!" everyone yelled and laughed.

"Because, motherfuckers, grief has gotten enough free rent!"

They started with food and beer, because that was easy. Frankie iced down cans in a cooler that still smelled faintly of shrimp. Lila lined bottles along the railing where the boards were flattest. Dottie looked until she found what she wanted—Bud in a bottle—and nodded once, satisfied. Henri brought a sack of ice over his shoulder like it weighed nothing and split it between coolers without asking. Yvette set out plastic cups, then replaced half of them with the real glasses from the kitchen, deciding it mattered.

Claudia set up a small cocktail station near the bayou, balancing a cutting board across two chairs. She mixed water lilies the way her sister had taught her, careful with the pour, lime squeezed hard, salt wiped from the rim with her thumb. Yvette watched once, then stepped in beside her, steadying the board when it shifted. Margaritas followed. No one kept count.

They ordered Mexican from El Rincon on Lemoyne Boulevard—paper bags sweating grease, tortillas wrapped tight, the smell of cumin and char drifting out before anything was opened. Henri carried the bags down the pier two at a time. They ate standing up, leaning on railings, passing containers without asking. Someone put music on low. Someone else turned it off again.

Frankie dragged a folding table onto the pier and Lila dressed it with butcher paper and the first strand of lights she found. Dottie made a list nobody read, but it calmed her down. Henri set the propane and checked the burner, then stepped back. Yvette kept cups moving and kept the glasses from tipping. The boil took over the yard the way it always does—steam, spice, and people drifting closer.

Claudia's arm was good enough for cracking claws. It still ached when she lifted wrong, but it held for this.

She set the mallet aside and used the heel of her hand, splitting shells clean, like she'd been doing it all her life. Potatoes went into the boil with corn and lemons and whole heads of garlic. Blue crabs went last, a rattle and a clatter, the lid shifting until the pot settled. Henri lifted it once, just to check, then let it be.

They ate until the table stained through and the paper tore. Later, they carried blankets onto the porch and slept there, doors open to the bayou air. Henri took the far chair. Yvette lay back with her hands folded, watching the lights until they blurred. They dreamed, or didn't, and woke with appetite.

The next day, they warmed up the leftovers and ate with their hands. Butter ran down wrists. The dogs collected what fell and lay full with their heads on their paws, watching women turn into little girls for an afternoon. Frankie tried to teach Lila how to two-step on the boards, but Lila insisted the boards needed the kind of dancing that listens to wood.

Somewhere near the porch, the playlist shifted on its own. The buoyant shuffle slipped, caught—and without anyone touching a thing—Johnny Cash's voice came through—low, late, wrong for a party: I hurt myself today.

No one reached for the speaker. The dogs lifted their heads. Butter shone on wrists. Paper plates sagged in the heat. The song ran its course and went quiet.

Frankie approached Claudia. "Too soon, hon?"

"No, it's good. Really. And thank you."

The group burst out with a laugh for Claudia because the world owed her a celebration that wasn't scheduled by sadness or regret. Caroline handed out paper crowns that Lila had made.

Dottie rolled her eyes like a queen who knew that she already ruled, that no crown was necessary. She lifted her glass, grease on her fingers, and said only, "For you, Claudia. And for your Mama."

It was enough—the table went quiet just long enough for the words to soak in, then the laughter rushed back like tidewater.

• • •

The golden afternoon rolled into evening. Frankie made a liquor run to her bar as the others helped Caroline and Claudia execute their promise to their mother.

The makeshift boat was nothing more than a shed door.

Frankie sanded it down. It wouldn't have to float very long once they lit it on fire.

Lila painted it clean, pale strokes giving the old wood a kind of dignity. On the prow, Claudia painted her Norse vegvísir. Henri and Yvette frowned, then started helping her, despite any Creole objections. They knew it didn't have to be the vevè the Toussaints so often used, tracing cornmeal or salt into dirt or porch floors.

"It's a Norse compass," Claudia explained. "Doesn't point north but toward safe return."

Yvette grinned.

At the center of this homemade Viking vessel, they placed a small urn, black clay polished smooth and etched with silver figures from Norse and Icelandic myth: Odin's ravens, serpents coiled into knots, runes carved for passage. Inside were the ashes of their mother.

Around the edge they ringed mason jars, scrubbed clear until the glass shone. Each was filled with lamp oil and a cotton wick.

Before they pushed the boat from the pier, Dottie crouched low and wrote a single name in neat script on the underside, where only the bayou would ever read it—the woman who had taught Claudia and Caroline how to hold a knife steady, keep a secret safe, and carry grief without letting it hollow them out.

• • •

Henri held the boat as Claudia stripped down and jumped into the bayou.

"C'mon Caroline!" she shouted as she dunked her hair in the dark water.

"Hell no," Caroline laughed. "I'm a chicken. You always swam with the gators. Not me!"

The water closed around her like a second skin—cool, heavy, and carrying the rank sweetness of mud and moss. It pressed into her, washing the last of his touch from her body. She thought of baptism, of birth, of the nights she had wanted to vanish into this same bayou and never return.

Now she swam not to escape but to guide. She took the boat from Henri and thanked him.

"You got this, cher?" he asked.

Her eyes brimming with light, she nodded.

The boat sailed toward her, and she guided it out toward the bay beyond the pier, the votive flames already lit.

Spanish moss dripped above her—tall bands of green and gray. Frogs worked their way back into the conversation. Something large moved in the reeds. Claudia laughed for the first time in months.

Flame flickered from jar to jar like a crown of stars. Lila led the others in murmuring the names of Caroline and Claudia's mother and father and let the water carry them.

Caroline stood at the edge of the pier, drink in hand, and watched with joyful tears as her sister spun the boat further out into the bay.

One by one, Claudia knocked over each mason jar, igniting the dried palmetto fronds that formed a nest underneath their mother's urn.

As the boat began to catch fire, she whispered something only the water could hear, a secret she had carried since the hospital bed, and felt lighter when the flames answered back.

Old aches and new strength sat together in them, not as enemies but companions.

Frankie, Dottie, Henri, Yvette, and Lila flanked Caroline, bare shoulders touching, butter still sweet on their fingers, smoke folding into their hair. The boat drifted toward the bend where the bayou narrowed and the world divided and then learned how to meet again.

Claudia thought of all the words she had been taught to say that had never once saved her. She thought of the pepper line and the documents and the drum. She thought of the day she'd promised her mother a sending rich enough to answer a life that had been taken in small bites until there wasn't enough left to feed.

Fire licked along the edge of the boat. The jars hissed and bloomed. The little boat shone brighter, then began to bow. No one on shore spoke. Neither did the house. The bayou did what water always does. It kept and carried.

Claudia lifted her chin toward the dark green arch that had become a chapel and answered the one voice in the world that would always make her listen.

"I'll miss you, Mama," Claudia said to the fire, as she turned and started swimming back to shore. "I'm sorry I took so long—but I'm here now."

Twenty-Five
JELLY JARS

By late September, Bayou House had started to breathe on its own again. The porch quit its constant groan. The front room no longer smelled like a wet hymnbook. Claudia and Caroline moved through the rooms with tool belts slung low, paint chips stuck to their arms like feathers after a storm.

They started with the bones. Sistered joists under the steps. Replaced the board where Henri's cornmeal vevè had been, just for good measure. Scrubbed the smoke off the kitchen ceiling, two summers of it, the kind that clung like a grudge. Caroline patched the bullet divot in the door frame with wood putty the color of café au lait. Claudia rehung the pantry door and replaced the broken sash lock in the back bedroom so it thunked shut with a clean, respectful click. Contractors began to arrive, replacing windows and sashes. The scent of tear gas, they knew, would linger for months.

Claudia's right arm still had a stubborn hitch to it—usable, not forgotten. Some mornings she could swing a hammer. Some mornings she just held the stud steady and let Caroline do the muscle.

They kept a new, more hopeful ledger on the icebox with a magnet shaped like a skull and bones: Salvage molding, a screen door Caroline had spotted at St. Vincent's thrift store, and a new fan belt.

They also listed seven gallons of "Heron" — white in the can, haint-blue once it dried. Ring shank nails at Henri's insistence.

On the rough mornings they made a pot of cold brew Café Bustelo and dosed it liberally, almost indecently with limoncello and half and half. On the better ones, after grabbing sausage biscuits from Hardees in D'Iberville, they worked in a quiet that felt chosen.

Word traveled that the porch was open again. Old neighbors started drifting back with armfuls—okra wrapped in newspaper, a chipped bowl good for gumbo, a box fan with one bent blade that still worked. Dottie turned up with a mason jar full of screws organized by size like a little universe. Frankie brought a length of cypress cut from a dock, already planed smooth. Lila arrived with a pack of hand-rolled incense that smelled like frankincense and the inside of an old cedar drawer.

They set flowers, cut fresh, pink, a little reckless, in some of their mother's jelly jars—and poured afternoon cosmos with vodka, Cointreau, and cranberry juice in the rest of the jars and stored them in the fridge. They learned how to make Caroline's favorite cocktail, the water lily, in a wide metal basin the color of moonmilk, with crème de violette, lemon, vodka, and simple syrup.

Smoke climbed lazy from a citronella coil and then switched to incense when the mosquitoes got bored of them; even the bugs seemed tired of bad news.

• • •

Sheriff Buck came by on a Tuesday, hat in his hands. He didn't park in the yard this time. He left the cruiser at the road like a man who understood boundaries. Caroline met him at the steps and didn't move aside until he balled up the courage to look her in the eye.

"Ma'am," Buck said to her, and the word wasn't the old Southern spackle, it was a swallow. "Ms. Marston," to Claudia, and he almost said more before he found the sentence he needed. "I'm so sorry."

He stood under the eave, hat clutched against his chest, sweat wetting the leather band. Claudia let him hold the silence long enough to prove he could, then lifted her chin toward the swing.

"Say it sitting," Caroline ordered. "Apologies tip over if you make them on your feet."

He sat. The swing complained and then accepted him. Caroline remained standing, arms crossed.

Buck cleared his throat. "I owe you both a hundred more, but I'll start with the ones I can, in order. We should've moved sooner. We should've believed sooner, knowing what our guts already knew. I was careful in the wrong direction. That's on me."

The newly glazed, wavy porch windows watched him suspiciously. The house did too.

"I do have updates," he offered. "You deserve to know where it all landed so far."

He took out a folded legal pad, but he didn't read it. He looked at Claudia instead.

"Ray's back in county lockup. Denied bond this time—flight risk and danger both."

"To himself or others?" Caroline quipped.

"Both. The DA's put five felony counts on him. Extortion, witness intimidation, assault, fraud. He'll have a forever if they add racketeering."

"His PD's already fishing for a deal," Buck continued. "But the state wants him to sing first. If he names people you'd recognize, it won't make him less guilty; it'll just give him some more roommates."

Claudia surprised herself, not even flinching at Ray's name.

"Two of his strays," Buck went on, "Haskins and the lanky one everyone calls Shoes—parole violations. They're back in too. The young blonde woman he kept bringing around—the thin one—she's gone. No forwarding address."

"Hope she got her car back," Claudia said, dry.

Sheriff Buck rubbed the back of his neck as if it ached from holding up a head full of regret.

"Trey Langston," Buck said, as Caroline blew out a small snort. "Took a plea. Financial misconduct, falsifying church records, theft by conversion. Three years, suspended, five on probation, restitution ordered. He's barred from handling money for any charity, church, or nonprofit in this parish. Pastor Reese—"

He looked up, measuring Claudia for a reaction; she gave him none and he continued.

"Pastor Reese got run out. There's talk he's in Slidell or Jacksonville. I don't care where he is so long as that scumbag's not here. The church board dissolved, and the new deacons are the kind who can count without being told who they owe."

"Well that's a start. And the Bayou Brotherhood Ministry?"

Frankie's voice came from the doorway. She'd padded out barefoot, a tea towel thrown over her shoulder like a flag of truce.

"Under investigation," Buck said. "But effectively dead in the water. The AG's office is holding that line. Some of the men from Gulfport who thought they were anonymous aren't anymore. A couple already lawyered up."

"And the casinos?" Dottie poked.

The Magnolia Crown and Sandbar Belle settled a consent decree in principle," he replied.

"So those fuckers are back open, aren't they?" she added.

"Pretty much," he said. "Their compliance officer found a job in Reno. Their CFO found Jesus in a press release."

Dottie let out a disgusted, elegant little laugh. "Filed between 'we categorically deny' and 'we look forward to serving the community better in the future.'"

"What about Margaret Ann Whitfield?" Caroline asked.

Buck rolled the hat brim under his thumb and pinched the edge until it squeaked. "

"Margaret Ann? Her husband shot himself before he could get himself indicted. Bank filed on the property. She's with a cousin in Hattiesburg."

Buck paused and swallowed hard. "I don't celebrate any of that," he said. "But that house ran on threats and checks for a long time. Now it's just… empty."

"Ends come in different sizes," Lila offered softly from the table, stirring vodka cosmos in a jelly jar like a small bouquet for a saint nobody could agree on.

"Isaiah Duvernay?" Dottie asked, more needle than thread in her tone. "Some motherfucker tried to weaponize Ice, but he's still a man. Don't lose him in your paperwork."

"Parole violation," Buck said, "but he cooperated. He gave statements that made some of this possible. Doesn't look like he killed the McKinnons, as much as everybody would like him for it."

"But it was a hit, though?" Dottie asked curiously.

Buck looked past the porch, past the yard, like the answer lived somewhere out by the water. "Confidentially," he said, and then corrected himself, quieter. "Off the record."

He rubbed the brim of his hat with his thumb. "Yeah. It was a hit. Not local. Dixie Mafia muscle brought in from out of town—guys out of Mobile and Pascagoula who don't stay long enough to be remembered."

Frankie's jaw set. "Ordered by who?"

"Money from Gulfport," Buck said. "Businessmen who liked the way the Brotherhood kept things tidy—debts quiet, permits greased, mouths shut. McKinnon stopped playing along. He threatened to talk about the books, about who was laundering what through which churches and which boats."

He swallowed. "They didn't want a warning. They wanted a punctuation mark."

Dottie nodded once. "And Ice?"

"Ice was noise," Buck said. "Useful noise. He scared easy, talked loud, fit a story people were already comfortable telling. The kind of man everybody's willing to believe is guilty."

"But you can't charge it," Claudia said.

Buck met her eyes. "Not yet. The case is a tug-of-war now between the state and the feds. Everyone wants it. Nobody wants to blink first. Too many names. Too much money. Paper's still moving."

"Anyway, Judge gave Ice time served and a slot in a carpentry apprenticeship through a church in Baton Rouge. Real church. He wrote you a letter..."

Buck patted his shirt pocket and then found it folded under the yellow pad. "Said to tell the ladies of the house he'd try to build something that stayed put."

Claudia nodded once. "That was nice."

"And me," Buck said finally, voice down in the boots of it. "I'm up for re-election. I don't expect your vote. I'm not here to ask for it. I'm here because I carried water for people I should've been hauling into a courtroom."

"We are sorry about your kid," Frankie offered. "How's he doing?"

"Chemo is working," he smiled hopefully. "Thanks for asking. But I know it made me look compromised as hell. And I know I left y'all to build your own perimeter defense. That's on me, and it makes me feel like shit."

Caroline spoke for the first time since he'd sat down. "We appreciate the update. You know... you don't have to be afraid of us."

Dottie bristled. "The hell he don't."

"Sheriff, if you're still around in the spring," she said, gesturing with her chin toward the basin, "You can come look at the lilies out here on the bayou. You don't have to knock. Just look.

"What she's saying, sheriff," Frankie said, "Is that these sisters here managed to keep Bayou House, in spite of all you motherfuckers."

"But the door is open," Claudia added, the faintest smile toward all four women surrounding her. "Thank you."

Buck stood. He didn't reach for a handshake he hadn't earned. He put the hat back on like a man accepting his own shade and stepped off the porch like you step off a boat into a current you mean to fight.

• • •

After Sheriff Buck left, Henri and Yvette arrived through the side yard, the ubiquitous copper bowl tucked under his arm. They sat at the long table and watched the light slide through the trees, slow and gold, catching the flies in a glitter that made even the nuisance look almost holy.

They poured sweet tea and then something less lawful into it. Lila's jelly-jar cosmos leaned toward each other, co-conspirators. Caroline passed her water lilies generously in their mother's fancier cocktail glasses.

Nobody rushed to talk. They told small stories—Miss Ida's rooster shut up by a hawk, a freezer of mullet that turned out to be catfish. The new librarian at Ocean Springs Middle School with a sleeve of tattoos that caused two decency committees to form and then accidentally date each other.

The sky went lavender then low blue, and a barge on the far water sounded its horn like a patient animal calling itself home.

Claudia felt the story roll toward her before anyone asked for it. She could feel Caroline's sideways look, the same one she threw across a grocery aisle when she saw their mother considering the expensive olives. Lila handed Claudia another jelly jar, and Claudia took a drink that burned in the good way.

"All right," Claudia said, settling back into the swing. "But to tell it right, I've got to start with the question that set the whole damn thing up…"

"The one about how your last relationship ended, right?" Caroline smiled.

"The brewery in Gulfport," Frankie added. "The speed-dating night."

Lila laughed through her nose; Dottie smirked.

"Fine! I'll tell it again!" Claudia surrendered.

"Again! Again!" they all laughed.

"Ok, here goes. So Bachelor One says, 'I'm between jobs but very spiritual.' Translation: unemployed with opinions on crystals. Bachelor Two asked if I'd ever considered moving to Panama because 'taxes are for sheep.' Bachelor Three called his ex 'crazy' before the foam on his stout settled—big, big red flag."

Caroline put two fingers to her lips and whistled the way their mother used to call dogs home.

"Then came the last one," Claudia rolled on, enjoying herself. "The headliner, or so he thought—a man with a leather cuff and the posture of a repentant bass player. He opened with, 'Full disclosure: I'm an empath with a dark triad past.' I said, 'Sir, those are opposite coupons and both expired.' He said he didn't believe in labels unless they were on bourbon. He asked what I did for fun. I said I color-code receipts. He said that sounded controlling; I said it sounded like I'd kept three small businesses from falling into a sinkhole."

The porch shook with the kind of laughter that loosens nails in a good way.

"He said he loved women who didn't 'need' him," Claudia added, "and I said I loved men who didn't make needing them into a personality. He told me he was writing a screenplay. I asked if it was about a man who grows up to stop telling women about the screenplay he's writing."

Frankie slapped the table. Even Yvette, apostle of few words, grinned into her tea.

"Anyway," Claudia said, "I checked three boxes 'no' and one 'are you in witness protection.' The hostess rang the bell like a fire drill. I got in my car, watched a couple make out like teenagers by the food truck, and I thought: red flags aren't cute anymore. That was the night before I let Ray back to the garage to get him out of the swamp the first time."

The laughter quieted on its own.

"So here's the moral," Claudia finished, "From a woman who ignored all the red flags: if a man tells you he's a miracle, count your change. If he says God sent him, check the till. If he calls every woman before you 'crazy,' look for the fuses he keeps handing out like candy."

They laughed again.

Later, after the others had gone, Claudia and Caroline walked the rooms of their parents' house in moonlight. The new paint glowed the quietest haze of haint blue. The patched door clicked. In the bedroom Caroline had claimed, a stack of library books waited, spines unbroken. In the kitchen the to-do list on the refrigerator had one new line: plant more lilies.

They stood in the doorway and listened to the tree frogs start their council meeting down in the ditch.

Claudia took Caroline's hand and squeezed it once. She thought of their parents over in Bellande Cemetery. The graves would remain, at times half-flooded, but new flowers stubbornly bright.

Plastic angels leaning at odd angles, wings furred with algae. She thought about what the water keeps, what it gives back, and how grief, like tidewater, never really leaves—just changes salinity.

"We staying?" Caroline asked.

"Yep," Claudia said. "I'm not going back to New York. Fuck it."

Outside, a row of jelly jars kept their flowers upright. The smoke thinned to the sweetness of honeysuckle. Out on the water, a shrimp boat made its way home, dragging a lace of fish nets.

They were home.

AUTHOR'S NOTE

There are maps that chart rivers, and there are maps that chart damage. On the Gulf Coast, they tend to overlap. The water keeps records better than people do. It remembers what was built on top of it and what was buried beneath.

It remembers the mills that bled into it, the refineries that renamed it after saints, and the sermons that promise cleansing but deliver debt. Every spill, every flood, every lie that runs off a roof or down a storm drain—it all ends up here, suspended in the same brown currents that nourish the Gulf.

Every town thinks its corruption is unique. But it isn't. Drive far enough and you start to see the pattern repeat: the same backroom deals, the same sheriff's cousins, the same sanctified real estate. The coast just happens to show its rot easily because water rises faster here. But the pattern runs inland too—through pine woods and paper mills, through mountain hollows and courthouse squares that still smell of bleach and sweat and paper money.

This book isn't about guilt or innocence. It's about what happens when systems—moral, civic, financial—go unexamined long enough to normalize their own damage.

What we often like to call corruption is often just the natural consequence of infrastructure left too long unexamined. The pipes rust, and we pretend the leaks are isolated events. But the system is always the story.

Exposure changes what can be denied. There's a grace in that. To trace a pipeline leak or a money trail is to see where pressure finally breaks. To name the damage is to begin a repair, even if the repair never holds.

Maybe that's all anyone can do—follow the water, watch where it rises and where it stains, and tell the truth, even if it hurts the ones you love or care about.

The South is full of those places: A refinery town on the Texas border. A coastal parish where the bayou glows at night. A mountain valley where the creeks run red after hard rains.

Each one believes its story is separate or unique. It never is. People still stand on porches and swear they didn't know. They always say it the same way.

Southern landscapes keep their own records. They carry what we build, what we break, and what we bury. And if you stand long enough on the edges of this world, you begin to understand the same truth that every river, mountain, coastline, and desert knows: nothing stays buried for long.

ABOUT THE AUTHOR

Douglas Stuart McDaniel is a writer of Southern civic noir whose work is preoccupied with what communities remember, what they bury, and what eventually surfaces anyway. His fiction moves through the fault lines of American life—coastal towns shaped by storms and silence, mountain communities bound by inheritance and omission, and cities where power learns to disguise itself as respectability.

Born in the shadow of the Appalachian Mountains and raised on fire-and-brimstone sermons, Cold War dread, and dog-eared paperbacks passed hand to hand, McDaniel is a Gen-X writer steeped in regional memory and moral consequence. His work is shaped by the South's long familiarity with contradiction: faith alongside corruption, hospitality beside violence, humor pressed into service as a survival skill.

For a number of years now, McDaniel has lived and written far from home: in the deserts of Saudi Arabia, the United Arab Emirates, and Jordan; in European and North African cities like Barcelona, London, Cairo, and Tangier; and across Brazil, Uruguay, and Argentina. He worked internationally for more than thirty years across infrastructure, urban systems, and global megaprojects. But these southern stories never loosened their grip on him. Distance sharpened them. Writing from outside the region gave him the clarity to return without nostalgia or apology—to examine how power works at ground level, how damage becomes normalized, and how loyalty operates independent of truth.

His Southern noir trilogy—*The Dark Water Gospel*, *Defiance: A Reckoning with the Dream*, and *Bloodwater*—forms a continuous investigation of place and consequence. Appalachia, Reconstruction-

era Savannah, and the modern Gulf Coast become linked terrains, each shaped by inherited systems of belief, money, and omission.

These are not stories of redemption neatly earned, but of reckoning postponed, negotiated, and sometimes refused.

McDaniel's previous work spans fiction, history, and film. His first novel, *Ghost Emperor*, a historical epic set in the chaotic decades following the death of Alexander the Great, traces the violent struggle over a collapsing empire where power, memory, and legitimacy are fought over as fiercely as territory. Alongside his novels, he has written multiple local and regional history books rooted in Western North Carolina, East Tennessee, and Savannah, focused on overlooked narratives, civic memory, and the lived texture of place. His work for screen includes three feature-length films, a range of short films and music videos, and a body of one-act historical plays developed with support from the Tennessee Arts Commission.

With Premium Pulp Fiction, McDaniel writes without pseudonym or protective distance. Premium Pulp Fiction authors are driven by the conviction that places remember, that history is rarely finished with us, and that some stories demand to be told exactly as they are.

He now divides his time between a home on the Mississippi Gulf Coast and his studio in Barcelona, Spain—writing at the edge of the places that made him.

Douglas Stuart McDaniel's
SOUTHERN CIVIC NOIR SERIES

Douglas Stuart McDaniel's Southern civic noir series forms a unified investigation across time and geography. Appalachia, the Lowcountry, and the modern Gulf Coast become linked terrains, each shaped by informal power, managed memory, and the long consequences of omission. The setting changes. The machinery does not.

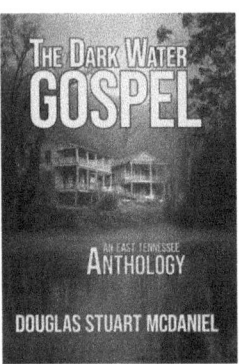

Set in East Tennessee, *The Dark Water Gospel* examines how civic power operates in small communities through omission, loyalty, and managed memory. Drawing on archives, court records, and lived accounts, the stories trace how decisions are made without minutes, how accountability is deferred, and how public language absorbs private misconduct. Like the work of Flannery O'Connor and James Baldwin, the book is less concerned with exposure than with process—how patterns of harm are reframed as isolated incidents, and how communities learn to live with what they refuse to name. The result is a civic record rather than an indictment, attentive to how power survives by appearing ordinary.

Set in Reconstruction-era Savannah, *Defiance: A Reckoning with the Dream* follows Reverend James Simms, a freedman and educator who mounts a campaign to become one of Georgia's first Black state legislators. The novel traces the legal, religious, and civic systems mobilized to block Black political power in the postwar South, focusing on how resistance was structured, justified, and quietly normalized. Similar to the work of Colson Whitehead and Edward P. Jones, the book resists heroic simplification in favor of institutional clarity, foregrounding the lived consequences of law, theology, and procedure. It is a study of how democracy is constrained in practice—and how its failures are later misremembered.

Set along the Mississippi Gulf Coast, *Bloodwater* examines how religion, incarceration, and coastal development intersect in a region shaped by selective accountability. When two sisters inherit a bayou house marked by violence and unresolved history, they are drawn into a confrontation with a charismatic street preacher—and the wider system that shields him. Echoing the civic noir of Attica Locke and the moral gravity of Jesmyn Ward, the novel is not a mystery of individual guilt but a study of how harm is absorbed, redistributed, and rendered acceptable. The Gulf Coast emerges not as backdrop, but as an active participant in the normalization of damage.

www.ingramcontent.com/pod-product-compliance
Lightning Source LLC
LaVergne TN
LVHW061614070526
838199LV00078B/7275